LITTLE LOVES

THE CHURCH DOGS OF CHARLESTON #2

MELISSA STORM

Editor: Megan Harris
Cover & Graphics Designer: Mallory Rock
Proofreader: Falcon Storm & Jasmine Jordan

Partridge & Pear Press
PO Box 72
Brighton, MI 48116

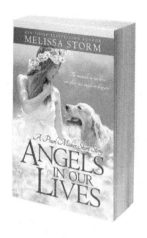

A FREE GIFT FOR YOU!

Thank you for picking up your copy of *Little Loves*. I so hope you love it! As a thank-you, I'd like to offer you a free gift. That's right, I've written a short story that's available exclusively to my newsletter subscribers. You'll receive the free story by e-mail as soon as you sign up at www.MelStorm.com/Gift. I hope you'll enjoy both stories. Happy reading!

MELISSA S.

To Sky Princess and Mila:
My own personal Chihuahua loves

PROLOGUE

PASTOR ADAM

Some say that whenever it snows in Charleston, God is giving a miracle to His most favorite of places. I tried to remember that as the cold reaching fingers of the wind poked and prodded my cheeks, nose, and everything else not already covered up by my scratchy winter getup.

But the more I tried to be optimistic about the shocking turn in the weather forecast, the harder that miraculous snow swirled. Soon it had bleached out the entire sky so that it was hard to tell where earth ended and the heavens began. We had a veritable snow storm on our hands just in time for the celebration of His birth.

I mumbled a quick prayer that those traveling tonight would remain safe and hugged my threadbare coat tighter around my shoulders. Head down, I fought against the wind, marching ever closer toward my destination.

Leave it to me to get so caught up in my Christmas Eve sermon that I'd forget my cell phone right there on the pulpit! Lucky thing I did, though, because as I finally reached the front doors of the sanctuary, I discovered a most disturbing sight.

Our locally famous nativity scene had been on the fritz all week, but now the angels' glowing halos had plum run out of power, casting the entire display into darkness. And on Christmas Eve, no less.

Ignoring the cold, which had found its way straight up underneath my clothes, I stepped closer to investigate the source of our power outage. Last summer old Mrs. Clementine had taken it upon herself to plant a little garden right outside the church. How could I say no to her request when she said all the food from our newly christened vegetable patch would be donated to feed the hungry?

And so with more than a little trepidation, I said *yes*, and unfortunately so did every little critter within a twenty mile radius. Even with the crops resting for the winter, I had no doubt that one of Mrs. Clementine's rabbit friends had tried to make a home of Christ's manger—and a snack of His power cords.

Upon closer inspection, I found that—yes, just as I'd suspected—a tiny ball of brown fluff had nestled into the nativity right there between Mary, Joseph, and the kindly shepherds who'd come to pay their respects.

Darn varmints!

Well, that's what I wanted to think, but then I stopped myself. These poor creatures hadn't expected the sudden snowfall either. They just wanted to get warm, and maybe God had sent me back to offer assistance on His behalf.

My toes began to go numb, but I tried to ignore that tingly sharpness as I stepped in for a closer look at the trembling animal.

Imagine my surprise when I found not just one creature, but five!

Right there next to the little Lord Jesus lay a mother dog and her four newborn pups. How they'd managed to survive this long was truly by the grace of God.

I didn't want to leave them, but I couldn't carry them all at once either. At least not on my own. After retrieving the box that our latest batch of hymnals had arrived packed inside, I stripped off my scarf and made a little nest. Then one by one, I lifted the mama and her puppies into the cardboard carrier and brought them into our church to get warm.

My lungs could scarcely take in a single breath of air until I made sure that each pup was alive and well. Only by the glory of God each of these tiny newborns moved just enough to show me they were okay. You must understand these dogs were hardly bigger than my own thumb. They could have easily been mistaken for rat pups if not for that brave mama dog.

A quick search on my newly retrieved phone confirmed that these were not just any dogs. They were the most diminutive of all dog breeds.

I didn't even stop to question why the Almighty had sent me five Chihuahuas in need as an early gift for His birthday. I didn't have to, because right then I knew beyond the shadow of any doubt these dogs were meant to find us. Surviving that cold Christmas Eve outdoors was only the first of many miracles that mama dog and her pups would bring to our congregation...

CHAPTER 1

HARMONY

Thirteen months later

Harmony King had been running for a long time. At first, she was always running toward something—more specifically, toward freedom. Growing up in the foster care system would not be how she'd chosen to start life, and she definitely wouldn't have elected to remain a slave to that system until her eighteenth birthday finally set her loose.

But that's exactly what had happened, anyway.

All those years as a little girl with no home to call her own, she longed to live life her own way, to be the master of her own fate. Somehow, though, she'd only managed to continue her lifestyle of drifting from one place to the next without feeling any real connection.

It made her wonder: was she *born* broken, or had that just happened along the way?

Because, no question about it, something was majorly wrong with her.

That was part of why she'd returned to Charleston. As much as she'd fought to escape the Holy City as a teen, truth be told, it was the only place she'd even come close to belonging.

Her homes had shuffled about faster than a magician preparing his cards, but a kindly agent at Child Protection Services had fought to keep her in the same schools growing up. It was the only constant she'd had up until that point.

When she could, she would sneak away to the Eternal Grace Church and listen to the pastor regale his congregation with tales of fortitude, forgiveness, charity. Jesus had been a poor wanderer, too—and Harmony liked that. It made him relatable, although when she'd mentioned this to her foster mother at the time she'd earned a cold, hard slap on the cheek and her fastest reassignment to date.

This experience strained her relationship with the church, but she still managed to attend services at least once per month by scraping together any spare change she could find to purchase a bus ticket that would deliver her to the service and hopefully, one day, salvation.

Sometimes she'd even pretend the pastor was her long-lost father and that one day they'd realize their relation and hug each other, sobbing big, ol' tears for all the time they'd already lost. But Harmony knew this was just a dream. She knew nothing of her birth father other than that he could have been any number of men. Her mother, who had been the very worst kind of junkie, died when Harmony was just four. But sometimes, if she clenched her eyes shut real tight, she could call up the memory of her mother's face.

And some other times she'd wish her mother had died much earlier. Because if she had, baby Harmony would surely have been adopted. Angry, dramatic four-year-old Harmony had tempted no one into taking such an action.

Of course, she often wished that she'd never been born, but then immediately prayed for forgiveness to the Almighty. As far as she was concerned, God had put her on this earth for a reason, and it was her failing—not His—that she hadn't figured it out yet.

Most recently she'd been living in Alabama, but when she'd lost her job and gotten evicted by her landlord, she knew her time was up in that particular locale.

It was always her tongue that got her into trouble. Harmony could put the fear of God into just about anybody, which had been a necessary skill to fight off the unwanted advances of foster brothers and fathers, along with a fair-sized collection of schoolyard bullies, too. But it was also a skill she couldn't control even now. If someone made her angry, they were going to hear about it—and with colorful language to boot.

She was sure God didn't mind. The two of them had an understanding when it came to these things, but Harmony still wished she could learn a bit of discretion. It certainly would make her life easier. At least a little bit, anyway.

There was little she could depend on in this world, but God always came through in some way or another.

That was another reason she'd returned to Charleston now—to the church where she'd first discovered her faith, to the pastor she'd liked to imagine was her father, to the only place she'd really stayed long enough to form some good memories along with the bad.

And, oh, did she need those good memories now.

She needed answers, too. Some kind of direction she'd yet to find in her nearly twenty-eight years.

Harmony dipped her head in reverence as she stepped into the sanctuary of Eternal Grace. After a quick glance around to confirm that she was alone, she did the only thing left to do. She dropped to her knees and prayed like her life depended on it. *Dear God. I need you. I'm so afraid...*

CHAPTER 2

HARMONY

Harmony prayed so long and so fervently that she all but lost track of time. When at last she lifted her bowed head, opened her eyes, and swiped at the tears that had flown freely down her face, she saw that she was no longer alone in the sanctuary.

"God's got ya," the same pastor she remembered from her youth said with a kindly smile and a quick nod. "Whatever it is, He knows, and He'll take care of you, too."

"Th-th-thank you," she stuttered. The embarrassment of being caught mid-prayer sent a sudden flash of warmth straight to her cheeks.

The pastor sank down a few seats away from

Harmony and folded his hands in his lap. "Miss Harmony, it has been quite some time."

"You remember me?" She eyed him cautiously. Just how much *did* he remember, and why did he actually seem happy to see her now? Of all God's eternal mysteries, Harmony always found it most suspect when someone from her past welcomed her back into their presence with open arms. It had only happened a handful of times, but the most recent had been such a spectacular disaster that this situation now with the pastor gave her pause.

Pastor Adam carried on without even the slightest hesitation. He'd always had the gift of gab. Only he practiced it in far better ways than Harmony used her own version of the same... gift. "Of course I remember you. I've thought about you many times over the years, wondered how you were doing, sent up prayers. It's good to see you now."

"I didn't know where else to go," she confessed with a shrug. If she acted like this wasn't a big deal, then perhaps it wouldn't be. Then again, that ship had likely already sailed when she decided to flee her last home in the early hours of that morning and drive straight up to Charleston, with only the odd break here and there to use the bathroom and stretch her legs.

Pastor Adam smiled consolingly in that same way he always had whenever speaking of the disadvantaged, and Harmony King was definitely one of the disadvantaged—now more than ever.

"You did right by coming here. You're always welcome at Eternal Grace." He waited for her to say more, but when she didn't, he added, "I'm still an exceptionally good listener if you'd like to talk about what's troubling you."

Harmony thought about this. She liked Pastor Adam—trusted him, too—and yet her burdens felt too big to offload onto somebody else. In truth, she already knew that only God could save her now.

"I never found talking about my problems to be an effective method for solving them," she said with a sigh. "Instead, they just seem to shine a spotlight, make 'em that much uglier."

He chuckled softly. "True enough, Harmony. True enough."

They sat in companionable silence for a few moments, leaving Harmony to wonder if she might just excuse herself and head home for the evening—provided she could find a spare room to rent somewhere near to here.

Then the pastor spoke again. "Of course, you shouldn't tell me anything you aren't comfortable sharing, but it's been a long while since I saw you last and I'm mighty curious… What have you been up to all these years?" He watched her expectantly, hopefully, but she already knew that anything she chose to reveal about her life would surely come as a tremendous disappointment.

"I left the very first second I could," she told him without even a single shred of regret.

He nodded, keeping his eyes fixed on his hands folded neatly in his lap. "I remember that. It's why I've always wondered how you got on. Worried, too. Eighteen is awfully young to forge out and make a life for one's own."

"Yes, it was. After Charleston, I went up north. First to Tennessee, then Ohio. I worked as a waitress mostly, because I couldn't afford schooling." Harmony had gotten good at skimping on the details when presenting herself to others. She needed to say just enough to get the job, to snag the rental, but never too much. That would only make them suspicious, make them turn her away. For all of Harmony's misfortunes, she was still a decent person, but folks who hadn't been in her shoes often missed that small, important point.

"So you were in Ohio until now?" Pastor Adam continued, pushing her along slowly as was his way.

"Gosh, no. I've been all over the place. Every time I lost my job for running my mouth, I'd pack up and move again. But I never found a place that felt more like home than Charleston." She marveled at how her old accent had come back out in full force. In all her travels, she'd never lost her Southern accent but had often adapted it to fit her current region rather than her roots.

"What brings you back now?" The pastor's questions kept coming, and they were beginning to wear Harmony out.

"This time I wasn't just running away. I was running from something, too. Or rather someone." She shouldn't have said that. It was too much for anyone besides her to know.

The pastor didn't gasp or suggest she call the police. He merely nodded and said, "But running all the same. Are you here for good now?"

"I can't say for sure. It's hard to put down roots when the very nature of your childhood is hopping from one house to the next. It doesn't take long for my feet to start itching, wanting to journey somewhere new, see what else is out there." Yes, it was easier to pretend she wanted this life, because that made it easier to accept.

"I hope you find a reason to stay," the pastor

confided. "And if you need any help, I'm happy to provide it. A home, a job, you tell me what you need, and I'll find a way to deliver. With His help, of course." He pointed to the ceiling and smiled.

"Thank you," she mumbled. "That means a lot."

She almost asked if he knew of a room she might rent, but if the last two years had taught her anything, it was that she should depend on herself—and only herself—to get things done.

She'd prayed that Alan would never find her, that he wouldn't hurt anyone else either, that she could find a way to belong and, like the pastor had said, a reason to stay and make her home in Charleston. She'd asked God to deliver her from the repercussions of her own mistakes, to once again set her free.

But she already felt the walls closing in, moving fast toward the Holy City, trapping her in the only kind of life she'd ever known and erasing any last vestige of hope.

CHAPTER 3

HARMONY

Harmony twiddled her thumbs, spinning them in circles around each other. She was ready to leave the church, but the pastor stayed sitting quietly in her company. She was just about to excuse herself when at last he spoke again.

"Actually, if memory serves, you never were good at accepting help from others," he said, scooting closer to her with a knowing smile as if she'd suddenly been found out. "And I reckon that hasn't much changed."

"No, sir." She grinned, though it was strange speaking to someone who knew her well enough to call out her habits. It had been years since anyone had figured her out. Well, anyone besides Alan.

They shared a good laugh, although Harmony was beginning to feel rather discomforted by the exchange. The longer she stayed, the sooner the pastor would see through her, the sooner the final pieces to which she so desperately clung would shatter, thus leaving the puzzle of her life wholly unsolvable.

"Well, in that case," Pastor Adam said, rising to his feet and motioning for Harmony to follow him. "I'm not going to wait for you to ask for help. I'm just going to up and offer it right now."

She followed obediently as he led the way to his tiny church office, but she still argued against his offer all the same. "That's very kind of you, but I'll do just fine on my own. I really should be going. It's getting—"

"Just you wait one second now." He retrieved his phone from on top of his old, wooden desk and motioned for her to shush. His thumbs worked the digital keyboard quickly and deftly for a man of his generation. After a couple minutes of silence, he slid the phone back into his pocket and smiled over at Harmony.

"There. Now that's taken care of, let's have a chat."

Harmony blinked hard. If she wasn't careful, she'd

be trapped talking to the goodly pastor for all of eternity. *"Another one?"*

A deep chuckle rose from his belly and shook his growing midsection. Age hadn't been the kindest companion to Pastor Adam, but Harmony saw right away that the same honorable man she'd always known resided within the puffier, wrinklier exterior. "Yes, another one. Or, rather, a more specific one. Come."

He led her out to the church foyer where they now waited within spitting distance of the front doors. "I just spoke with my daughter, Abigail. Do you remember her?"

Harmony nodded. "Yes, we had some classes together. She was always nice to me."

"Good to hear it." He pulled out his phone again and shook it demonstratively. "That was her I texted just now, and well, she's on her way here."

"She's coming *now?*" She'd only wanted a place to pray, clear her head a bit, and regroup. She hadn't meant for this quick church trip to turn into a whole big thing. But such seemed to be the Charleston way and Pastor Adam's in particular. She figured his own personal motto should be *if it's worth doing, it's worth overdoing.* This afternoon was clearly proof of that.

"Right now." He tossed his phone from hand to hand, catching it each time but worrying Harmony he'd drop it and crack the screen all the same. She cringed at the memory of all the good phones she'd lost being careless.

The pastor must have caught her discomfort, because he suddenly stopped and dropped his phone back into his pocket. "And she's bringing Muffin," he said with what looked like it may have been a wink.

"That's nice of you both, but I'm really not hungry. I need to—"

He laughed again. "Not muffins, Muffin. Your new dog."

"Dog?" Well, that couldn't be right. Why on God's green earth would Pastor Adam think she needed or wanted a dog?

He eyed her so contentedly after delivering his announcement that she had to put an end to this crazy notion immediately.

"No, no, no. I think there's been some kind of mistake."

"Well, he's really more of a loaner dog, but—boy howdy—do you two need each other." He was dead serious about this, and she was dead set against it.

"I'm not really in the position to..." She let her

words trail off. If she explained that she didn't yet have a job or a place to stay, then the pastor would no doubt spring to further action, call in more favors, keep her hostage until he was absolutely certain that she was fully provided for.

"Please," he said firmly and with a sad smile. "You need comforting, Harmony. You need someone who understands and won't ask too many questions. I'm only human, but Muffin, he's a certified therapy dog and one of God's most special miracles."

This assertion shocked her into silence. Didn't therapy dogs stay with their trainers? Why would the pastor—who hadn't seen her in nearly ten years, by the way—thrust a dog on her mere minutes after becoming reacquainted? It just didn't make any sense.

"This dog… Muffin… is a miracle?" she asked slowly to make sure she understood him right. Ten years was a long time. Perhaps Pastor Adam had gone crazy since she'd last seen him. Anything was possible, after all.

"Sure as I'm standing here. Have you heard the story of our church dogs before? It's been about a year since they found us now, a very good year."

"Um, no," Harmony said. *Don't appear ungrateful,* she reminded herself, *but don't get suckered into taking a dog, either!*

Pastor Adam stood straighter and spoke animatedly with his hands. He'd clearly told this story many times before. "It was two Christmases back—like I said, just over a year. I forgot my phone at the pulpit after delivering the Christmas Eve sermon. When I went back—"

"Are you only telling Muffin's origin story just now? I'd have figured that would be the first thing out of your mouth." The pastor's daughter, Abigail, swept into the foyer with a baby on her hip and two tiny dogs walking beside her on leashes.

Harmony hadn't even heard her come in, such was the volume and the vigor of Pastor Adam's storytelling.

"Dad says you and Muffin are *destined* for each other," Abigail said with a big roll of her eyes. "Told me I had to be over lickety-split before you could second-guess things." She pressed a leash into Harmony's palm and closed her fingers around it tightly before stepping back and regarding Harmony with a grin. "So, here you go, this is Muffin."

The little dog barked, perhaps to say hello, perhaps because he was equally confused about their sudden arrangement. One thing was for sure: Pastor Adam really, really wanted her to have this dog… and how could she say no to the man who had given her so much over the years?

Well, crud. It looked like Harmony had herself a dog.

CHAPTER 4

HARMONY

Harmony stooped down to let the fawn and white Chihuahua sniff her hand. She'd been around enough dogs growing up to know that this little gesture of peace went a long way when it came to convincing a dog not to bite you.

Not that the pastor would foist a vicious dog upon her, but still… up until a few minutes ago, she hadn't expected him to foist any dog upon her at all.

Muffin licked her hand enthusiastically and didn't stop lapping at it until Harmony pulled back.

"She sure is friendly, but I'm afraid I don't know much about dogs." There it was, her final attempt to say no. Too bad she already knew it would fall upon deaf ears.

"Muffin's a *he*," Abigail corrected. "I know it sounds a little silly, but the Sunday school kids named all the puppies, and—well—they went with a bakery theme. Someday I'll have to introduce you to his siblings Cookie, Brownie, and Cupcake."

"And who's this?" Harmony looked toward the other dog who sat at attention beside Abigail. It was plumper than Muffin, but otherwise looked very much the same.

"This is Muffin's mother." She stared at both dogs lovingly, as if they, too, were her children. "We call her Mama Mary. You know, since she gave birth in a manger?"

Harmony couldn't contain her laughter. Truly she was in the presence of the holy family—or at least the canine version of it.

"You arrived just as I was getting to the good part," Pastor Adam said to his daughter, then jumped straight back into his animated tale of how the Church Dogs of Charleston had come to be.

By the time he reached the end, Harmony suspected her jaw might be hanging wide open. Even though it was terribly rude, she just couldn't help herself. This litter of pups had been through a lot, almost as much as Harmony herself, but she still didn't understand one very important thing...

"I can see they're an incredible group of dogs, but why do you want to give one to me? Shouldn't they stay with the church?"

"Not giving, *loaning,*" the pastor corrected with a wag of his finger. "And Muffin is staying with the church. He's staying with you. We both know that the church is made up of people, not bricks and mortar. Keep coming back each Sunday, and maybe Tuesdays, too, for a bit of counseling. What say you, Miss King?"

She glanced down at her feet hidden within a pair of old, dirty Converse she'd had for ages. Harmony felt torn between considering the dog a kind gift and a terrible imposition. Perhaps Muffin would prove to be both.

"It's okay if you don't know dogs," Abigail said when no one else spoke. "I can teach you. In fact, if you're up for it, little Owen, Mama Mary, and I were just about to head to the dog park for a bit of exercise. I'm sure Muffin would love to accompany us, too. What do you say, Muffy?"

The little dog barked and wagged his tail so hard that his entire body shook. Maybe a doggie companion wouldn't be the worst thing in the world, but so far Harmony had been given far more questions than she'd received answers.

"I'd love to come, but what do I feed him? And won't he miss his family? And how often does he need exercise? And... well, I'm sure there are a million more questions I don't even know to ask yet." It all made her head spin. Did they really think she could take care of another life when she could barely manage her own? Why were they willing to take such a risk on her when she'd only just gotten back into town? Something didn't add up.

Abigail and Pastor Adam both chuckled.

The pastor placed a warm hand on Harmony's shoulder. "I wouldn't have asked you to take Muffin if I didn't think it would be the best decision for both of you. These pups have worked miracles before. It's what they were born to do. Let Muffin do his job. Let him help you. He's a good dog, and you deserve him. After all, the Lord works in mysterious ways, and lately, in the case of Eternal Grace, that's through these little shivering balls of fluff."

"And for a more direct answer to your question," Abigail said as she fished through her oversized shoulder bag and pulled out a stapled bundle of papers. "Here's your guide to caring for one of our church dogs. The answers to all your questions are right in here along with my number. Call me any time. It's my job to take care of these pups and to run the program. I'll be visiting you throughout the week to check in and make sure you are both getting along. I also have a care package waiting for you in my car. It has Muffin's favorite foods, toys, blankets, pretty much everything you need and then some."

"Welcome back to Charleston, Harmony," Pastor Adam said, holding his arms open to request a hug.

Harmony eagerly stepped into them and felt the warmth of his non-judging, omnipresent love.

"Welcome home."

As Harmony looked to Abigail, her adorable son, and each of the dogs, she saw that roots had risen up from the earth to anchor her to this city.

At least for a little while longer, at least for now, it looked like she'd be calling Charleston her home—and Muffin her roommate.

CHAPTER 5

PASTOR ADAM

As I live and breathe, I never expected to see Harmony King set foot in Charleston again. She was always a kind child, but so, so broken. It wasn't just the lack of a family that got her started off all wrong. The kids made sure she never forgot what she was missing.

I often encouraged my daughter, Abigail, to reach out to her, but she insisted that it would be social suicide to have the girl no one liked come to our house for a bit of food and kindness—no matter how much the poor thing needed both. Abigail herself never made matters worse for Harmony, but I often wonder how much it would have meant to that poor girl to have a stable friendship to lean on for support.

Of course, I still remember the first time she was

shifted about the system. I was certain that she was lost to Eternal Grace forever, but she had an angel on her side working at the Child Protective Services. That angel kept her nearby enough so that she could attend church and stay in Abigail's class at school.

No, she didn't make it every Sunday after that, even though I suspected she might like to. I offered to pick her up before first service and drop her home after second, but she never agreed to accept my help. I suspect she didn't want to depend on anyone if she could help it, and I can see she's still very much the same.

That's why I entrusted Muffin to her.

Oh, I saw her hesitation, the fear that she was now responsible for another life when she'd barely figured out how to manage her own, but God doesn't give us more than we can handle—I know that for a fact. And from the very moment I set eyes on Harmony praying like her life depended on it, there in the middle of my mostly empty sanctuary, God leaned in real close to my heart and whispered, "This girl needs a miracle. Let's give one to her."

And around here, "miracle" is just a fancy word for "Chihuahua." Yes, Harmony needed our church dogs in her life. Mostly because she needed someone she could count on, and I suspect she's never quite had that before. She needs to learn to forgive those involved in what happened to her—hard as it may be —and she needs to learn to look forward to better things, let others in to enjoy them with her.

But for now?

A dog will do just fine.

More than fine—*miraculously*.

A little love can go a long way. Now it was up to Muffin to answer God's call and finally give Harmony the chance to live a life to His glory as well as to her own satisfaction.

God speed, little Muffin.

And God bless.

CHAPTER 6

HARMONY

Harmony hopped in her old clunker and followed Abigail out of the church parking lot and toward a nearby dog park. At the pastor's insistence, Muffin rode along with Harmony, sitting proudly on the passenger side seat with his tongue lolling straight out of his mouth.

Less than five minutes later, they pulled into a small parking lot outside of a hilly fenced-in area. It was a good bit of space for being so near the heart of the city and appeared to be lovingly cared for, too.

Oh, the things people would do for their dogs.

Would Harmony soon be a doting dog mom herself? She had to laugh as she pictured dressing herself and Muffin in matching outfits and carrying him around town in a designer shoulder bag.

No, that vision belonged to somebody else's life. It would never be part of Harmony's.

"Told you it wasn't a far drive," Abigail called, standing outside her car and waiting for Harmony to extract Muffin from the inside of hers.

Unfortunately, before she could figure out how to grab him and pull him out of there, the little dog evaded her reach and leapt straight out onto the ground where he ran in tight, crazy circles around her ankles.

Harmony bent down to grab him from the parking lot, but the little dog was still too quick.

Abigail laughed. "That's okay. He knows the way in. C'mon."

Together the two women, baby, and the more mild-mannered mother Chihuahua headed into the dog park.

"Looks like he may be taking advantage of your inexperience," Abigail explained, but she didn't seem too worried about it. "Muffin knows better than to act without waiting for orders first. Lord knows he's had more than enough obedience training. It's okay, though. It just means that I may have to drop in three times a week to start until Muffin learns to respect you as his new pack leader."

Harmony nodded along passively, even though

she secretly worried that this little dog was quickly becoming her full-time job. How would she pay for rent or food or anything else if every waking moment was devoted to helping Muffin so he could, presumably and supposedly, help her?

The questions kept piling up, and they were beginning to give her a headache.

Abigail must have caught her worried expression, because she placed a consoling hand on Harmony's arm and said, "I know it must seem overwhelming right now, but believe me, soon it will all be a routine. One you'll love more than anything. Trust me, I was exactly where you are hardly more than a year ago, and I thought my father was crazy for taking in these five dogs out of nowhere, but he was right to do it. He was right about everything."

"The dogs helped you… um, *what* exactly?" Harmony asked, hoping she wasn't coming across as rude. Abigail and the pastor were both trying to be kind and help her. The last thing either needed was her signature ill temper to make the situation that much more difficult.

Abigail smiled and swept her gaze across the horizon. Both Chihuahuas were running so fast their feet barely connected with the ground before lifting up again. A handful of other dogs roughhoused nearby, but all seemed happy and friendly despite the muffled growls that rose into the air above the park.

"Remember to live," Abigail said thoughtfully. "That's what they helped *me* with. It might be different for you, though. Oh, sure, I didn't believe it at first either, and I can tell from your expression you've got more than a couple doubts about the situation, but just… trust it, okay? Can you do that?"

Harmony shrugged, and when Abigail's face crumpled she quickly turned that shrug into a nod— a hesitant one, but agreement all the same. The two women hadn't been close growing up, and Harmony doubted they could be close now, but it did seem like the pastor's daughter wanted to help.

"How long have you been married?" she asked, groping for a change of topic in hopes Abigail wouldn't pry deeper into her life or the events had heralded her return to Charleston.

"What makes you ask that?" Abigail responded, keeping her eyes glued to the Chihuahuas as they jumped into the fray with the bigger dogs.

Harmony pointed toward the baby. "You said this is Owen, right?"

Abigail's face fell, but only for a moment before she righted it again. "Oh, right! Well, I'm not married at the moment, but I am engaged. Just recently, as a matter of fact. Do you remember Gavin Holbrook from school?"

She pictured the tall, handsome jock from her youth. Many of the girls had harbored not-so-secret crushes on Gavin, but not Harmony. She'd talked herself out of crushing on anyone back then, and she wished she'd have continued the habit into adulthood, too. There never was any use setting herself up for future disappointment.

Still, she was happy for Abigail that she'd managed to find a small bit of happiness in this crazy world. But she was also a fair bit confused.

"Didn't your father raise a fuss about you being unmarried and—?"

Abigail rushed to correct her. "Oh, no, no, no. That's a whole big story. I'll tell it to you sometime, but today is about you and Muffin, not about me and little Owen here."

"Ok-ay," Harmony said slowly, stretching the word apart into two long syllables. Even though she was curious, she knew it wouldn't be fair to press the other woman about her past when she herself wanted to keep everything in her life a secret.

"But first, can I ask you something?" It seemed she needed a fresh topic change again, and her visit to the church had taken up far more time than she'd planned. It was time for Harmony to ask for help—better Abigail than the pastor, she supposed.

Abigail turned to her with a warm smile that looked so much like her father's. "Sure. You can ask me anything."

Harmony tried not to flush with embarrassment. She hated asking for help, but occasionally it was necessary. "Do you know where I might be able to rent a room for the next couple months?"

There, she'd done the needful and casually committed to at least sixty days in Charleston, and with Muffin at her side. It probably wasn't the worst thing in the world. She just hoped she wasn't compounding one mistake with another.

CHAPTER 7

HARMONY

Harmony listened as Abigail told her all about an older church lady who was in need of some company and had a room to spare. It was decided that the two of them would pay her a visit straight after the dog park, with the dogs and baby in tow.

Frankly, it was rather amazing how she'd only been in town for a couple of hours and already had a dog, a place to stay, and maybe even a friend. But that was Charleston for you. Most of the time, the people were so friendly it almost seemed suspect. Harmony had learned to no longer question the kindness of strangers. Instead, it was the known folks from her past who gave her pause.

After some time the mother Chihuahua, Mary,

came back to rest in the shade of the park bench beneath them. Muffin, who had far more energy left to burn, found a stick along the fence line and began running in wide looping circles around the park to show all the other dogs his prized find.

One dog in particular took a special interest in this charade and gave chase. Of course, it was the biggest, scariest looking dog in the entire park—a lanky, gray behemoth with wiry hair and coal eyes. He had to have at least fifty pounds on Harmony and would probably be taller than her, too, if he were to stand up straight on his hind legs.

Had they been on the street, she would have crossed to the other side for safety. Instead, this great beast was galloping after her brand-new borrowed dog, and the last thing Harmony needed was to see that poor little critter get mauled to death right before her innocent eyes.

"Hey, Muffin! C'mere, doggie!" she called in a high-pitched, childish voice, bending forward and patting her knees, praying the dog would listen for his own good.

And he did… but so did the other dog, who came lumbering after.

"Hi, Pancake!" Abigail cooed. She didn't even

need to bend forward to stroke the massive dog between his ears.

"Pancake?" The name seemed ludicrous, not a good fit for the massive dog at all. Not really the best name for any dog, if she was honest. "Are all the animals around here named after foods or what?"

Abigail laughed as her baby blew spit bubbles and reached toward Pancake with chubby hands. "Just our church dogs and, of course, this big guy here." She used a baby voice that made all three dogs wag their tails wildly with excitement. Even Mama Mary woke back up to join in the fray.

Harmony took a step back as Pancake flopped onto the ground and rolled on his back. "He's massive," she said with a shiver.

"Yeah, Irish Wolfhounds get pretty big. Pancake is actually on the smaller side, believe it or not."

"I choose not," Harmony quipped. Why would anyone want a pet that could so easily overpower them? At least her loaner dog was small and easy to carry around if needed.

A tall, slender man spotted them from across the park and came jogging over. "Sorry about him!" he called. "He always loves it when he gets a chance to play with little dogs. He didn't slime you, did he?"

"Hi, Nolan. No, we're fine. It's good to see you and Pancake," Abigail answered for the both of them.

Harmony quietly studied the man standing before her. She vaguely remembered the pipsqueak two years behind her in school who was also called Nolan, but this fellow looked nothing like him at all. He was at least six foot five with long, lean limbs, sandy blond hair, and a smattering of freckles splashed across his thin nose. The thing that made him truly handsome, though, was his shining green eyes, which studied her with amusement.

"Have we met?" he asked, offering her an ingratiating smile. "I feel like I'd remember meeting someone as breathtaking as you."

Oh, brother. Harmony had been hit on plenty of times. Men liked her curvy figure and long, dark hair that fell halfway down her back in tight waves. Pickup lines that included *breathtaking,* however, usually came from men far older than Nolan. Honestly, this smooth-talker was nowhere near as impressive as his hulking beast of a dog.

"That depends," she answered cautiously. "Are you Nolan Murphy?"

His slow grin seemed oversized for his face. "None other. It seems my reputation proceeds me, then."

"Yeah, it's not that." She looked away to hide a smirk. It was a special pleasure of hers to keep male egos in check. "We went to school together."

"You remember Harmony King, don't you?" Abigail prompted.

Harmony saw the exact moment recognition flashed in Nolan's emerald eyes. "Oh, you were the girl—"

"Without a home, yeah. That's me. Hi." It always sounded worse coming from someone else's mouth, which is why Harmony chose to beat him to the punch instead. From pickup lines to punch lines, it turned out this would be a very memorable trip to the dog park, after all.

Nolan frowned and twisted his hand in his dog's shaggy fur. "That's not what I was going to say, but forget it. Who cares about the past when we all live in the present?" He winked at them, and Abigail fell apart in friendly laughter.

Harmony remained silent. The longer this conversation continued on, the more awkward she felt. Why wouldn't Nolan just take his dog and go back to his side of the park already?

"I haven't seen you in ages," Nolan told her, smiling once more. "Are you newly back in town?"

"Very newly," Abigail answered for her.

"Well, welcome back," he continued as if it were perfectly normal for someone else to be carrying on Harmony's side of the conversation when she was standing right there herself. "Maybe I can take you out some time, show you how things have changed?"

Harmony shook her head and looked away. "I don't think so, Nolan."

"Oh, okay. Have a nice day, then." Thankfully, he turned away without pressing for any further explanation as to her rejection.

Abigail frowned but didn't pester her, either. Nolan was the literal last man on earth Harmony wanted to date, other than maybe her ex, Alan. It might not have directly been Nolan's fault, but it was his sister—his very flesh and blood—who had made school especially hard for Harmony. Megan Murphy was the meanest of the mean girls, and she never let Harmony forget where she'd come from or where she belonged.

Which was to say nowhere.

She hoped it wasn't a bad omen that she had found a Murphy so soon after returning to town...

CHAPTER 8

HARMONY

Harmony stood beside Abigail as she rang the doorbell beside the large mahogany door fitted with stained glass panels.

"Just you wait. I'm coming!" an older voice called from inside. A moment later the door eased open to reveal a woman with white-blonde hair on her head and a string of plump pearls around her neck.

"I have a boarder for you, Mrs. Clementine," Abigail said, immediately handing her baby to the older woman who immediately broke out in an enormous grin.

"Well, isn't that nice? And you must be her." The woman turned to Harmony and stuck out her free hand in greeting. "Name's Virginia Clementine, and who might you be?"

"I'm Harmony. Thank you for agreeing to take me in," she mumbled. No matter how many times she rented a spare room from some widowed blue blood or middle-aged blue collar, it never got any less embarrassing as she was first getting settled. She felt like an imposter that day, just as she always had in the past when rotating between foster homes as a child.

"Honey, you're the one doing me a favor. It's been awfully lonely since Mr. Clementine took his promotion earlier this year. They have him on a new plane across the country just about every single week. How do you like that?"

Harmony nodded and smiled. She didn't know the first thing about working jobs that would actually pay for you to travel. From the looks of the grand hall before her, the Clementines earned a pretty penny for their troubles.

Some *trouble*, seeing the world!

"Muffin's coming with her, too. I hope that's all right." Abigail motioned to the little dog who'd already started sniffing around the cupboards in search of a spare crumb or some other such dog-approved treasure.

"That'll be just fine," Virginia said. "Any chance you'll be leaving little Owen, too?"

"Not a prayer," Abigail answered curtly, and both women laughed as if falling cue cards.

"I'll just go get Muffin's things," Harmony said, feeling like the odd one out in what was supposed to be her new home, however temporarily.

It took two trips to get all of the Chihuahua's things inside and only one to grab her own. Figured.

"Let me help you take these upstairs," Abigail offered.

"It's my old sewing room," Virginia instructed as she rocked the baby back and forth with wide, bouncing steps. "Just at the top of the stairs."

Harmony's new room turned out to be pretty nice, one of the nicest she'd stayed in in quite some time. The queen-sized bed was fitted with what appeared to be a homemade quilt, and she wondered if perhaps Virginia had made it herself to help stave off a loneliness she'd felt for longer than she'd initially let on. A large bay window looked out onto the backyard which was lined with palmetto trees—the official state tree of South Carolina, if memory served.

"I'll just give you some time to yourself," Abigail said, leaning up against the doorframe. "Unless you need anything?" The other woman seemed almost hopeful that Harmony would ask her to stay, but she needed nothing at this time and some solitude might do her good.

"Thanks for all your help today," Harmony answered with a small smile.

The other woman hesitated, then strode forward and gave Harmony an impromptu hug. "I know you've been through a lot and that you aren't telling us everything just yet, but I want you to know that I'm here for you. My father and Mrs. Clementine, too."

And with that, Abigail padded out of the room and latched the door shut behind her.

Everyone seemed so eager to help Harmony now that she'd returned to their lives. Was it because they wished they'd have done more when she was still living within the Holy City? Perhaps, but the course of Harmony's life was already set. Any form of lasting happiness surely wasn't within reach, but at the very least she could get by without any new and lasting pains, either.

A life of small mediocrities wasn't much to strive for, but it was the best Harmony could hope for now.

She sat down on her new bed, finding it pleasantly springy. It was then she remembered that in all her praying, she'd forgotten to thank God for the giant blessing he'd given her. "Thank you, Father, for helping me flee. Thank you for blessing my journey and delivering me to safety."

For there was no doubt in Harmony's mind now that she was safe here with these people who wanted to help and would protect her if any real dangers were to find her hiding here within this giant plantation-style house.

Trouble always did have a way of finding her out when she least expected it, but this time she would be ready.

CHAPTER 9

HARMONY

A scuffling sound came from the closed door, and Harmony rose to open it. Muffin trotted right in and stood on his hind legs. begging to be picked up. He looked like a very tiny, very un-scary modern-day T-Rex, which instantly endeared him to her.

"C'mere, you," she said, reaching for the five pound package of fur.

Muffin let out a shrill bark and scurried under the bed, then ran out of the room with a piece of cloth clutched in his jaws. Harmony chased after him as he ran down the staircase and into the living room where Mrs. Clementine sat sipping a glass of sweet tea as the television played softly in the background.

"Abigail, Owen, and Mama Mary just left," the

old woman explained. "And I'll be turning in for the night soon myself."

"Oh, okay," Harmony answered. It seemed mighty early for bed, but who was she to judge? Old people were just more tired, and while her new land-lady didn't seem exceptionally old, she did appear to be worn down by life more than her fair share.

"Mind if I give you the grand tour first?" Virginia asked with a slight raise of one eyebrow.

"Yes, please do." Harmony waited as the other woman grabbed a thick coaster with a cartoon pig dancing on its front and set her tea down on top of it.

"All right," she said, rising to her feet and drifting in the direction of the kitchen. Muffin ran after her, still carrying the cloth in his mouth and shaking his tiny head every few steps as if he could kill what wasn't even living.

Harmony sped up and grabbed the dog, then took what turned out to be a lace doily from his clutches.

Virginia laughed. "Oh, let him have it. I have a million and one spares lying around this place. God never blessed me with children to call my own, and instead of getting mad or sad, I just picked up a needle and thread." My, she did reveal the source of her pain right up front. Harmony was never so bold when meeting new people. Did it mean Mrs. Clementine trusted her, or was this simply her way?

"The quilt on my bed is beautiful," Harmony said with an encouraging nod. "You do great work."

"It beats sitting around wondering why the Lord chose not to bless me with one of life's greatest gifts. I figured I might as well find some other way to make the world a nicer place, and so I added a bit of beauty."

Harmony didn't know whether to smile, apologize, or reach for a change of topic. Luckily, Virginia shifted into tour guide mode, freeing her from the burden of figuring out an appropriate response.

"Cups are in there." She pointed to the cabinet next to the fridge. "This drawer is for silverware." She pulled a drawer in and out demonstratively. "This arrangement is for room and board, so please eat and drink whatever you want. I always have way more than I need just for me."

"That's very kind of you, Mrs. Clementine," Harmony said. She felt like she was back in school. *Yes, Mrs. Thank you, Mrs.*

The older woman waved Harmony off. "Call me Virginia, or better yet, Ginny. Some folk even call me Gin. C'mon, now let me show you where all the bathrooms are."

Harmony followed Ginny around the house for the next half hour trying her best to commit everything to memory, but mostly just offering a listening ear and a bit of companionship. By the time the tour ended, Harmony was more than ready to call it a day. To think it had started before dawn with a six-hour-plus drive up to Charleston, then there was the church, the dog park, and now her new home. She'd left one man behind and refused another.

And still, she didn't know what was next for her. Well, at least she had a solid foundation for figuring it out tomorrow with the first light of a new sun.

Muffin followed her upstairs to her room. Somehow he seemed to know that he belonged with her. Maybe in some ways animals were smarter than people, after all. This little doggie kept close watch over his new mistress and immediately hopped up onto the bed beside her and cuddled in beside her hip.

Today had been a good day, she decided, and for that she was endlessly thankful. Tomorrow could be an even better day just as long as she remembered to keep her expectations low and her mind open.

A new life was waiting for her. She just had to keep being brave and mindful of her limitations. If

God had wanted something else for her, surely He would have given it to her by now.

It was okay, though. It would all be okay.

Harmony closed her eyes and stroked the Chihuahua's smooth fur until at last she drifted off into a deep, comfortable sleep.

CHAPTER 10

PASTOR ADAM

I opened my eyes wide the second the sun peeked over the slight hill in our yard. As the years piled on, I'd begun waking up earlier and earlier. I often joked with Abigail that soon I wouldn't need to go to bed at all.

Yes, the wee hours of the morning suited me perfectly for my own personal prayers and reflections. There was something so special about being alone with God the Father before the rest of the world woke up and started making demands on the both of us.

After a quick hello to the Lord and a bit of reading in my Bible, I decided it would be a good time to call Mrs. Clementine to check on our weary traveler. As always, my old friend picked up after just one ring.

"It's like you know I'm calling before I do," I told her with the first smile of the day creeping across my face.

"I reckon perhaps maybe I do," she answered, a common exchange for us. Despite her oddities, I'd grown quite fond of my church secretary over the years. Truth be told, before Abigail returned to town and little Owen and the church dogs joined us, too, Virginia Clementine was the closest thing I had to actual family living in Charleston. She'd always seemed grateful for my company, too, and I was happy that the Lord had found a way to help her right along with Harmony.

"How is she?" I asked when Mrs. Clementine didn't immediately offer up the information I sought.

"She's still sleeping upstairs will little Muffin," she whispered. "Whatever happened to that poor child?"

I shook my head. "She only seems like a child because we're getting so old these days, but I do remember her when she was in school. That was before you'd joined our congregation. Almost ten years ago."

"She's very well mannered." She dropped her voice a couple of notches before continuing on. "But I'm afraid if I even raise my voice too loud in surprise she'll wind up cowering in the corner."

I couldn't stop the sigh that escaped me. "Harmony was never one to back away from a fight and I doubt that's changed now, but still, I don't like hearing how plainly she wears her pain."

"Actually, I think it's the pain that wears her." A soft tinkling of wind chimes sounded on Mrs. Clementine's end of the conversation, and I pictured her sitting on her back porch with a hot mug of tea in her hands. Morning was the only time she deigned to drink it warm. Tea, she always said, was meant to be served iced cold and with a good pound of sugar. I could scarcely argue with logic like that.

I fired up the coffeemaker for myself so I could join her with a beverage on my end of the line. "God brought her back into our lives for a reason, but I haven't figured out what that reason is just yet."

She laughed at my feeble attempts to understand the problems of a young woman like Harmony. "You mean God hasn't shown you yet. Honestly, Pastor Elliott, sometimes I wonder if it shouldn't be me up there giving the sermons each Sunday. You have a way of getting so deep in your meddling that you forget to wait for God to show His hand."

"And you, Mrs. Clementine, never hesitate to call me out."

She clucked and I could picture her sitting up

straight with pride in her wicker chair. "Well, goodness, somebody's gotta do it. Might as well be me."

We chattered about church business for a few moments before saying goodbye. As hard as it was, Mrs. Clementine was absolutely right. The only thing we could do for Harmony now was to wait.

Wait and pray.

And add a little love, too, while we were at it.

CHAPTER 11

HARMONY

Harmony woke up much later than usual the next day, and in those precious first moments between sleep and consciousness, she lost all recollection of the events that had taken place the day before. Her heart picked up speed as she opened her eyes, then relaxed again when the memories came rushing back.

Muffin, of course, was there to lick the corners of her eyes and the insides of her ears, whining with joy as he did.

"Well, good morning to you, too," she said, patting the dog on the head and offering him a weary smile.

Muffin took this opportunity to lick inside of her mouth, too.

"Gross!" She brushed the Chihuahua aside with a sweep of her arm and used the other to wipe vigorously at her mouth and tongue.

Muffin jumped off the bed and went to scratch at the door impatiently. Oh, right. He probably needed to pee. Harmony did, too, but at least she could be trusted not to mess on the carpet. So she grabbed a cardigan from the top of her suitcase, draped it over her shoulders, and led the little dog downstairs.

Her new landlady was nowhere to be seen, but the clock above the stove informed Harmony that it was nearly ten o'clock. The rest of the world was probably already at work for the day—and that included Mrs. Virginia Clementine, too.

Her stomach grumbled as she eased open the sliding glass door and let the little dog run out into the palmetto-lined yard. He, of course, chose the very largest tree to do his business, lifting his leg proudly to splash the base of the thick trunk and then shuffling his hind feet like a cat trying to cover up a mess in its litter box.

Does he miss his brothers and sisters? Harmony idly wondered and for a moment felt jealous of her new companion. This little dog had more of a support network, more of a family than she'd ever had even for just one single day in her life.

Lucky little thing.

She sighed and leaned back against the house as she watched Muffin entertain himself by alternating bouts of sniffing with fast, flying leaps around the yard. When he'd seemed to tire himself out, she let him back inside and took him up to her room.

"You're going to be on your own for a little while," Harmony informed him as she pulled on her nicest pair of pants and a button-down shirt. "I need to go find a job so I can afford to pay for your kibble."

Muffin sat down on the edge of the rug and womped his tail on the ground.

"How do I look?" she asked him after dragging a tube of lip gloss across her lips and posing for her reflection in the mirror.

The Chihuahua tilted his head to the side and released a shiver so fierce that he practically fell over from the sudden motion.

"I don't think I speak your language just yet. Any chance of you learning English?" She should have felt ridiculous, carrying on a one-sided conversation with a dog, but Harmony actually found it quite comforting to have someone who would simply listen without forcing his opinions onto her.

Muffin tilted his head to the other side, ran in a

tight circle, and then went back to scratch at the door.

"Sorry, Muffs. You've gotta stay here for now, but tell you what—if I do manage to find a job today, I'll bring you back a big bone to celebrate."

In response, Muffin dropped his tail between his legs, pressed his ears back against his head, and went to sulk under the bed. That was how Harmony felt about the situation, too, but she needed a job to keep her mind busy just as much as she needed it to pay the bills.

She and Virginia hadn't discussed the rental amount last night, meaning Harmony wasn't sure if she even had enough to cover the first week, let alone a few months or more of letting the room. The sooner she had a job, the sooner she'd have one less thing to worry about.

Please guide my steps today, she prayed silently as she passed halfway through the kitchen and paused near the fridge. After a quick debate on whether or not she should fix herself a bowl of cereal, she decided it was best not to impose upon Mrs. Clementine's kindness until she knew she'd have a way to cover the expense of her room and board.

With that decision made, Harmony's stomach grumbled again. It would have to make do with a handful of breath mints from the stash she kept buried somewhere in her purse.

"I'll find something. I will," she told her reflection in the rearview mirror. Desperation had a way of producing results, after all, and Charleston had hundreds of restaurants. Surely one of them would be in need of an experienced waitress.

Now all she had to do was keep her big mouth in line and remember to smile—*smile nonstop, never stop smiling.*

Harmony frowned at herself in the rearview mirror. Perhaps to get it out of her system, or perhaps because some part of her knew that trouble would find her no matter where she went, no matter how far away she got from Alan.

The best she could hope for was to delay the inevitable—and to find herself a job.

Here goes nothing…

CHAPTER 12

HARMONY

Harmony drove downtown and parked on the street in the first open spot she found. After using the last of her quarters to feed the meter, she began to search for an eatery that was hiring.

In the past, Harmony would have extended her hunt for a new job to the many retail shops that lined the city streets, but a few years back she'd faced such abuse from an unhappy customer that she'd vowed to only work at restaurants from that day forward. It didn't help that she'd told that rude customer exactly where she could place her non-returnable item—and it wasn't back in the box.

Oh, bless that bitter woman's heart!

She'd chosen downtown for her search not just for the variety of choices, but also because she preferred to avoid franchise restaurants if she could. Harmony had been through many jobs in the nine years since she'd set out on her own and had a fair number of rules when it came to selecting a good one: check the reviews on Yelp to make sure people like the food, order a meal to make sure they have good reason to like it, choose a place that's one of a kind even if it's a bit of a hole in the wall, and—most importantly—never date a coworker.

If there was one thing Harmony went through faster than jobs, it was dates. Maybe it was because she'd been waiting so long to have a family that she needed to make sure any man to whom she gave a permanent spot in her life fit said spot just right. Maybe it was because she was truly better off alone. Whatever the case, men had always disappointed Harmony, and she rarely gave them more than three dates to prove they weren't the one.

Alan had been the one exception. He'd hung on for nearly a year. Problem was, he didn't know when to let go. And even when Harmony suggested it was time to say goodbye, he dug his heels in and refused to let her leave.

Well, she sure showed him. She'd not only left

their town, but she'd also put the entire state of Georgia between them for good measure.

Bless his heart, too!

Okay, she needed to stop mentally blessing everyone's hearts before she worked herself into total and irreversible agitation. Introducing herself to perspective employers when she'd already worked herself into a rage wouldn't suit her end goals one bit.

She popped another breath mint into her mouth and shoved the nearly empty container deep into her purse. Slow, centering breaths brought her back to a place where everyone's hearts had not been personally blessed and the birds once again sang merrily from their hidden perches within the trees and rooftops of the colorful buildings downtown.

Across the street a little window sign read "Now Hiring" in big, red letters. *Yes!*

Harmony looked both ways before jaywalking her way over to the other side. She never once took her eyes off that sign for fear it might up and disappear before she reached it. Now that she was standing right in front of the place, she did a quick Internet search.

"O'Brien's, Charleston," she murmured to herself as she typed the text into her browser. The Yelp reviews were good, an average of four-point-seven stars. The prices were mid-range and the hours were six to twelve. Every single item on the menu was related to breakfast—some offerings were classic and others she couldn't even begin to picture from the ridiculous-sounding names.

Whatever the case, it seemed like a good place to apply. If she worked here, she could get her hours in early and then spend the rest of the day however she pleased.

Perfect.

She pushed into the dining room and took in the bright interior with freshly upholstered booths and shining tile floors. The place appeared close to empty now that closing time was only an hour away. She hoped it was much busier during peak hours, but right now, beggars couldn't be choosers—and Harmony was definitely a beggar.

"Good morning, darlin'!" a blonde-haired, big-bosomed waitress called from behind a pot of coffee. "Go ahead and take a seat, and I'll be with you in two shakes of a lamb's tail."

Harmony strode across the dining room. Her shoes squeaked on the tiled floor but she tried not to feel embarrassed. "Actually, I'm here about the help wanted sign."

"Oh, that!" The woman, whose nametag read Jolene, returned the coffee pot to its warmer than brushed her hands on her apron as she grinned up at Harmony. "It's been there forever."

Harmony forced a smile until it hurt. "Are you not hiring anymore?" she asked as if the answer didn't have the power to determine her future happiness.

Luckily, Jolene talked fast and freely, putting Harmony's doubts aside almost as soon as they'd surfaced. "Oh, no. We are! We'd just kind of lost hope. That is, until you showed up. What's your name, sugar?"

Harmony introduced herself to Jolene, all the while wondering if this would be the easiest job she'd ever landed. It seemed the waitress was ready to hire her based on the fact that she'd simply shown up and asked.

"Well, Miss Harmony King, the boss isn't in today, but he trusts my opinion and he likes everybody besides. If you want the job, it's yours." Jolene caught her reflection in the stainless steel backsplash behind the coffee counter and fluffed her hair.

Was it really going to be this easy? Harmony shifted awkwardly from one foot to the other. "Um, don't you want my references or employment history?"

Jolene waved her off. "Nah, those don't matter so much. The best way to find out if you've got what it takes is to put you on the floor. Be here at five thirty tomorrow and we'll get you started."

They shook on it, and Harmony jotted down her number and address on the back of a placemat just in case Jolene needed to get in touch with her before then. That was all it took to put even more roots down in Charleston.

It hadn't been this easy in a long time, and Harmony knew her streak of good luck couldn't last. Yes, the coffee cup was definitely half-full, but at least she had something to drink.

CHAPTER 13

HARMONY

Harmony returned to the house and pushed her new key in the lock. A joyous fit of barking sounded from just on the other side of the door. Had Muffin managed to escape her room? She hoped he hadn't destroyed anything in the short time she'd been out, especially since she'd kept her promise and brought him a rawhide to celebrate her new job at O'Brien's. She'd also ordered a bit of takeout for herself so she could try out the restaurant's fare for herself before peddling it to customers.

When the door didn't open, she twisted the key the other way and gave it a good jiggle.

When finally she gained entry, she found Virginia waiting in the entryway. "Oh, I never lock it. I suppose I should, but I've always found it best to believe the best of others."

She chuckled, and Harmony bit her tongue. It was as if the old woman were rolling out the welcome mat for any robber within a hundred mile radius. Luckily, Harmony herself had nothing worth stealing, especially among all the many beautiful things the Clementines owned.

"I found a job," Harmony informed her, then told her the story of meeting Jolene at the diner.

Muffin stood on his hind legs with his head pointed straight up at Harmony's purse. A small whine escaped his throat and interrupted Ginny's story about that time when Jolene had botched her own baptism as a youngster.

"Sorry," Harmony said with a sigh. "I promised him a treat to celebrate the new job, and I guess he can smell it waiting for him." She pulled the rawhide from her purse and removed the shrink-wrap plastic. The thing was practically as big as Muffin himself, but he had no trouble picking it up and trotting off to enjoy it somewhere in peace.

Virginia shrugged into a pretty baby pink jacket. "I need to get back to the church. I just stopped in for a quick lunch break. By the way, you don't need to leave Muffin cooped up in your room all day. I know him and the other church dogs quite well and don't mind giving him free rein of the house. Same goes for you. Consider this whole place your home, not just that tiny room upstairs. Okay, I best be off. Bye!"

Harmony said goodbye, then headed to the kitchen to pour herself a glass of water and grab a fork for her omelet. She took everything back up to her room and sat cross-legged on her bed as she ate. While she appreciated Virginia welcoming her into her home, she also found the hospitality to be a bit overwhelming. Harmony had always found it far easier to belong in a small space—her room, her corner, her bed—than to have too much space in which to roam about. More space meant more chances for trouble, more chances for finding yourself in someone else's space, and that someone else becoming downright angry about it.

That's how she'd first met Alan. His first words to her had been, "That's where I sit." And those words were quickly followed by a sharp elbow to her ribs.

They'd both found themselves in one of those homes that collected foster kids like it collected head lice. What could one more hurt? And so they'd opened their home to Harmony and their wallets to the check from the state that came with her.

At the time there were four others, mostly older boys who could be put to work around the house and yard as needed. Alan was the youngest of them and it seemed he was grateful to finally have someone under him in the pecking order.

He'd been terrible to Harmony, but that had only lasted three weeks before he ticked off their foster mom and was sent packing. She never thought of him again until she randomly bumped into him in Mobile, Alabama a little over a year back. He'd apologized a blue streak, saying he'd been an angry kid but he was a different man now—a better one.

And Harmony believed him, partially because she understood the anger and partially because she had no reason not to. They began to seek each other out more and more until at last Alan had kissed her straight on the lips and declared himself in love.

For whatever reason, she believed that, too. Not only that, but she told him she loved him as well. And for a few glorious months she'd thought all the pieces of her life were finally popping into place. She and Alan spent every free moment with each other, and because she was happy, she kept her tongue in line and managed to keep her job for a record period.

Then he went and ruined it by asking her to move in with him.

The request surprised her as the notion didn't seem at all romantic. They'd both grown up tripping over several other kids in cramped rooms that should have only bunked two tops. Harmony liked having a space all to herself, and she wasn't ready to give that up yet.

Besides, moving in together would invariably lead to pressure to have sex, and she had long since promised God she would wait until marriage. It was a deal they had made when she was growing up. She'd asked God to keep her body safe from hands that would hurt her or take liberties not due to them, and in exchange, she would remain celibate until the day she decided to become somebody's wife—provided that day ever came at all.

Of course, Alan made the situation even worse by asking her to marry him later that week. She wasn't ready for that, either. Didn't he know she was still trying to learn to take care of herself properly? There was no way she was ready to double that burden by joining her life with someone else's on a permanent basis.

She'd politely declined, but in so doing had drawn a jagged red mark through the timeline of their relationship. The good times were all behind them, and what was to follow would only get worse by the day. This is what confirmed it for Harmony. People didn't change. Alan hadn't tossed aside his anger; he'd only buried it deep down.

And she'd foolishly come along with a shovel.

CHAPTER 14

HARMONY

The next morning, Harmony turned up at O'Brien's twenty minutes early for her shift. She always found it best to be extra punctual in the beginning so that her employers would forgive occasional necessary tardies later on.

Jolene was nowhere in sight, but the kitchen light appeared to be on. Harmony rapped gently at the glass.

A shockingly tall man emerged from the back and approached the door with squinted eyes. "Harmony?"

"Good morning, Nolan." She recognized him by his height more than his face. "Do you work here, too?"

"Own it, actually." He unlatched the door and let her slip inside. Thank goodness she'd discouraged his interest in her at the dog park a couple days back. Otherwise she'd have had to quit right there on the spot.

"Thank you for hiring me," she said, glancing around for something she could do both to prove herself useful and to escape Nolan's watchful gaze.

"I didn't hire you. Jolene did." He pointed toward the industrial-sized coffeemaker. "Want to get that started?"

"Oh, yeah. Yeah, sure." Coffee she could do. Working so close to someone she found so handsome, well…that had yet to be determined. The last thing she wanted after the whole ordeal with Alan was another relationship, especially with someone she already knew to be from bad stock. If Megan Murphy had tormented her all through school without ever feeling guilty about it, then her brother's moral compass couldn't be much better. It didn't matter that he was trying so hard to charm her now. His tune would swiftly change once her rejection sunk in.

"I'm glad she did, by the way," he called after her with an amused lilt in his voice.

At this point, her inner thought train had pulled so far out from the station, Harmony couldn't even remember what the two of them had been talking about. When she turned, he was still watching her from the same place by the door where he'd been standing before.

A small smile crept across his face and turned ridiculously large, like that of a little boy who hadn't quite grown into his features yet. "How's Muffin doing?" Nolan wanted to know.

Harmony shook her head. "What?"

"Your new dog?" There was that smirk again, the same smirk that seemed to imply he found her both tiresome and adorable. She did not like it one bit.

"Oh, right. Well, I'm only borrowing him for a spell, but he's doing just fine." She reached up to tuck a stray curl behind her ear.

Nolan's eyes lingered on her as she attempted to work.

"Am I doing something wrong?" she demanded, spinning around and placing a hand on each hip as she glowered at him. "Because you're kind of staring."

Oh, no, not yet! Rein in that temper. You can't afford to lose this job over something so silly as a man looking at you.

He laughed and shook his head. "Sorry about that. I'm just surprised you're here is all."

"Didn't Jolene tell you she'd hired me? I gave her all my information. Look, if this isn't going to work, I can go right now." She prayed he wouldn't call her on her bluff.

"Whoa there!" Nolan put both hands up in front of him as if he were dealing with a spooked horse. "Jolene had your information but accidentally misplaced it. She couldn't remember your name exactly, only what you looked like." He blew out an exaggerated puff of air. "But that's Jolene for you—great with people, terrible with names. When she described you, I had a sneaking suspicion, but I didn't know for sure until you turned up."

"Well, here I am, turned up and ready to work." She snapped the coffee basket back into place and pressed the brew button. "What do you need next? Should I check the condiment caddies? Refill the ketchup bottles?"

He stayed rooted to the spot and his eyes glued right on her face despite Harmony's constant moving about. "You sure know your way around a dining room, don't you?"

"I've done this rodeo before, but I kind of find it hard to work while I talk, especially while I'm still learning the ins and outs of someplace new." She crossed her arms over her chest and frowned.

He cocked his head, the same as Muffin liked to

do. "So I need to stop distracting you. Is that what you're implying?"

"It's what I'm outright saying... sir." She added the sign marker of respect after an unnaturally long pause, but it seemed the best way to remind him of their positions. Surely he wouldn't want to date an employee, especially if O'Brien's actually needed the extra help as badly as Jolene had claimed.

He crossed his arms over his chest and studied her for a moment without speaking, then he licked his lips and said, "Why don't you take a few minutes to get acquainted with the menu? Jolene will be here soon, and then she can walk you through the rest."

She nodded and paced her way back toward the hostess stand to grab one of the oversized menus, then sank into the nearest booth and opened it up.

Nolan watched her every movement until he finally—*finally!*—returned to the back of the house to work on getting the kitchen ready for breakfast.

Though she did her best to learn the ingredients in each dish, the words blurred before her eyes. The last time a man had paid such close attention to her, it had turned into the stormy relationship that had sent her running straight out of Alabama.

CHAPTER 15

PATOR ADAM

When I called Mrs. Clementine this morning to check in on our visitor, she informed me that our girl had found a job working at O'Brien's. Seeing as I hadn't treated myself to a meal out in quite some time, I decided to pay her a visit around about eleven o'clock when I knew most of the crowd would be cleared out and she'd have some time to talk.

"Morning, Pastor Adam!" Jolene Brown called with two giant heaps of pancakes stacked high on her tray. "Take a seat and I'll be with you in a moment."

I waved hello and then took a seat in a booth toward the back of the restaurant.

Harmony found me not two minutes later. "Virginia told you about my job," she said, tapping her fingers at the edge of my table before grabbing a little notepad from her apron and a pen from behind her ear. "What can I get you to eat?"

I declined the menu she offered. "Whatever you recommend," I told her with a smile I hoped she'd find reassuring.

She scrunched her mouth to one side, then said, "I don't know enough to recommend anything, although judging from the rush today, our French toast seems to be quite well received."

I laughed. French toast at an Irish restaurant—of all the things! Well, to each their own. "That sounds great," I told her. "How has your first day been?"

Harmony shrugged. "Good enough, I suppose."

I nodded. Harmony had never been the effusive type. She'd always had to be drawn out a bit before she would freely share what was on her mind. "And how are you and Muffin getting on?"

She couldn't hide the small smile that spread to her lips. "Better than I expected."

"And Mrs. Clementine?"

"A very gracious host."

I raised an eyebrow. *"But?"*

"What makes you say there's a but?"

"Well, there aren't a lot of other words you're

saying, so I figured just maybe something was holding you back."

She sighed, glanced back at the kitchen over her shoulder, and then took a seat across from me in the booth. "But I have no idea what comes next," she confided.

"Folks worry too much about tomorrow. Just live today the best you can and tomorrow will take care of itself."

Harmony bit her lip. Was it to keep from saying something she thought I wouldn't appreciate? "You're right," she said after a moment. "Of course, you're right. Um, I should get back to work."

She didn't give me the chance to argue, and before I knew it, she had skittered off to the back of the house. Jolene brought me my French toast several minutes later, and I didn't see Harmony again the entire duration of my breakfast.

"The new girl a friend of yours?" Jolene asked later when she was refilling my half-full coffee mug.

I let the steam warm my face, inhaling the rich, earthy scent. Normally I didn't drink caffeine so late in the day, but partaking in a proper sit-down break-fast without a mug of coffee to go with it just might qualify as a sin. "Mmm, from a long time back," I told her.

"That's good," the waitress said before dropping her voice a couple notches and leaning closer to my table. "Because it seems she could really use one."

"Can't we all?" was my response.

Jolene laughed as she swept away from my table, her full hips swinging back and forth. A lot of men about town liked those hips very much, but none had ever managed to nail down their owner for a lifetime commitment.

I finished my meal and drained the last of my coffee knowing full well I'd be up later than I'd normally like that night, then left a tip for each of them and headed out.

I'd made it halfway down the block when the door to the restaurant burst back open and footsteps pounded toward me. When I turned, I saw Harmony standing with her arms crossed against the cold.

"Thank you for all your help," she said. "You really help me to feel like maybe I do belong here after all."

"Ain't no maybe about it." I turned to face her right there on the sidewalk. "Welcome home, Miss King."

If I'd been wearing a hat, I'd have tipped it in her direction. But since I wasn't, I just smiled and carried on my way.

CHAPTER 16

HARMONY

At Nolan's instruction, Harmony flipped the open sign to closed and pulled the blinds shut. Her shift had been busier than she'd expected, but she'd fallen into a nice rhythm with Jolene and ended up with a handsome wad of tips in her apron by the end of the breakfast rush.

"Oh, hold the door!" Jolene called, hurrying toward her just as she was about to flip the lock. "Thank you, sugar. See you tomorrow!" And she was out the door before Harmony had time to question it.

When she turned back toward the dining room, she found Nolan wiping down the warming shelf and staring daggers—or more accurately, hearts and flowers—her way. "I told her she could go on early.

Carolina—that's her daughter—is home from college on winter break, and I know Jolene wants all the time she can get before she has to head back. Besides, it gives the two of us time to talk."

Harmony scratched at her elbow and glanced around the emptied out space. "You sure do like to talk," she mumbled just hardly above a whisper, but Nolan heard her anyway and let out a boisterous chuckle in response.

"As a matter of fact, talking *is* my favorite. You did a great job today. The customers loved you." His eyes fell to her mouth as if he wanted to say more but didn't know if it would be welcome.

Harmony scowled at him, but Nolan didn't seem to get the message.

"I thought about it all day, and I do remember you from our school days. You were the cool girl that didn't care what anybody else thought of her. I liked that about you even though I was probably too young to register on your social radar."

Harmony turned her back to him and let out a deep breath. He really had no idea. Of course she had cared what others thought of her. She was a teenaged girl, for crying out loud! And it was Nolan's own sister who had made her days in class almost as difficult as her nights in foster care.

Once Harmony had managed to catch the movie *Carrie* playing on a cable news channel in one of those very rare occurrences where she had a house to herself for the evening. After that, she had spent months praying to God that He'd gift her with the same psychic abilities with which she could defend herself.

Granted, Megan Murphy and her lackeys had never gone so far as to shower her in pig's blood, but she suspected that was because her wild, wicked tongue made them just a little bit afraid of her. However much they were or weren't afraid of Harmony then, it was enough to avoid any physical altercations and—quite thankfully—expulsion, too.

She turned back around and offered Nolan a gracious smile without saying anything. She didn't trust herself with words just yet.

Please stay quiet. Please stay quiet, she tried to whisper to him telepathically, but as it turned out, God still hadn't granted her Carrie's gift even all these years later.

"Would it be weird if the two of us had some breakfast together?" Nolan asked, coming out from behind the kitchen wall. "Because if you give me just five minutes, I could—"

"Yes!" Harmony said too loudly to be considered

polite. "Yes, it would be weird. You're my boss. You shouldn't be hitting on me or forcing me to talk when I've made it very clear I'm not interested. It's highly inappropriate."

Nolan's face fell. "I'm sorry if I made you uncomfortable. I just thought you could use a friend."

"Well, I can't. Okay?" She glared at him, wondering if she should cut her losses and run right then and there.

Her new boss just kept talking, and he kept being nice, too, which irked her to no end. "I can still make you breakfast, if you're hungry. You look like you could use a hot meal in you."

Something unpleasant bubbled inside Harmony, and before she knew it, she'd boiled over. She cursed at Nolan, then added, "Will you just leave me alone already?" Too late she realized that this was not how you talked to your new employer if you wanted to keep your job and, despite everything, she did.

Well, shoot.

If Nolan was angry, he did an admirable job of hiding it. Instead, his eyes softened and he asked, "Who hurt you so bad, Harmony? Who made you afraid of the world?"

His kindness in the face of her temper shook her

just enough to bring Harmony back to her center. "You really don't know, do you?"

"Know what?" he asked gently, risking a step closer, but only one.

"You may as well scramble up those eggs. This could take a while."

CHAPTER 17

HARMONY

Less than ten minutes later they were both sitting before steaming plates of that day's breakfast special: eggs, bacon, sausage, grits, and fried green tomatoes.

"Why is this place called O'Brien's if your last name is Murphy?" Harmony asked Nolan as she sprinkled a liberal dose of pepper into her eggs.

"So *now* you want to make small talk?" Nolan shook his head. "Because earlier when I tried to do the same, you kind of cussed me out."

Her face burned hot as he watched and waited for her response. "Sorry about that," she mumbled.

Nolan reached out and took her hand. After giving it a quick, friendly squeeze, he let go again.

"It's okay. I understand, and it's one of the things I like about you."

Harmony let out a sarcastic laugh. "That I'm mean?"

"That you're *passionate.*" His eyes widened as he said that last word to add an extra pop of emphasis.

"You think you know me, but you're wrong. I'm not passionate about a single thing on God's green earth. I just have a wicked temper."

"Well, you're fighting hard for something. Maybe it's time you figured out what that is."

She laughed again and set her fork down on the edge of the plate. "Next you're going to tell me you moonlight as a shrink. Wait, do you?"

"No, but I have a passion for people." So he was an amateur counselor then, or just had a profoundly unusual interest in Harmony herself. She didn't much care for either option.

"And I have a passion for avoiding people," she shot back with a grin. At least her wit didn't fail her when it came to Nolan Murphy, even if her judgment seemed to be somewhat on the fritz.

He took a giant chug of orange juice, then wiped his mouth with the back of his hand. "The O'Briens are my cousins. None of them wanted to devote their life to the restaurant business, so it fell to me."

"What?" So much for having her wits about her.

"You asked about the restaurant, and now you know. So then, I believe you were going to tell me something important, which is why you deigned to have breakfast with me."

She smiled despite herself. Nolan was wearing her down, which could prove to be very dangerous if she wasn't careful. "It's good, by the way. The food."

He nodded and took a bite from the center part of his grits where all the butter had pooled, turning it into an extra delicious treat.

Harmony did the same. By the time she worked up the courage to tell him her story, they'd both already finished their full and very generous servings of grits.

"You asked who hurt me," she said. "The simple answer is everyone. The more complicated answer is your sister specifically."

Nolan dropped his fork and it clattered onto the table with a *clink, clink, clink.* "Megan?"

"She was horrible to me. Never let me forget I was foster trash and that I was in that position because my parents didn't want me enough to stay alive and nobody else wanted me enough to give me a forever home. She called it a forever home like I was some stray dog waiting to be adopted from the shelter. Well, I guess she was right about that part." But, no, even dogs got adopted eventually. Harmony had remained without a home her entire childhood. She often wondered why they hadn't just euthanized her if she was really such a burden to everyone who crossed her path.

Nolan stopped eating and stayed stock still, then started shaking his head as if in disbelief. "I just...I had no idea. Did she hit you, too? Hurt you in other ways?"

Why did it have to leave a bruise for people to consider the abuse she'd been through real? "No physical violence, no. Only damaged me to my emotional core which, in my very humble opinion, is far worse."

Nolan crossed his arms and leaned back against the seat, continuing to shake his head, though he appeared to believe her now. "No wonder you hate me."

"I don't hate you," she said reflexively, realizing then that in some ways she did. Fortunately, this talk was helping her to get beyond those feelings—not too far, but it was a start. "Okay, I *did* hate you, but I kind of hate most people. Don't take it personally."

His eyes fell to her mouth as he asked, "Do you hate me still?"

"You gave me a job." She shoved a forkful of eggs

into her mouth as soon as she spoke those words, hoping to turn his attention elsewhere.

And his unblinking gaze moved to her eyes. "That's not what I asked."

Harmony finished chewing and swallowed hard. The eggs had gone cold on her tongue. "No, I don't hate you, Nolan, but I don't share your interest, either."

"Because of my sister? I'm sorry she made school hard for you. She did the same thing to me, too. We weren't close then, and we aren't close now, so please don't assume I'm anything like her."

She took another bite to avoid talking. What else was there to say?

Nolan seemed to have it figured out. His eyes flashed with something she couldn't quite identify, then he said, "Would it help if I told you she dropped out of college and works as a cashier at Publix and is generally a very unhappy person?"

"No, seeing as I never went to college, am newly hired as a waitress, and am as unhappy as they come." There she went acting ungrateful again. She was happy to have the job, but she needed Nolan to lose that light that shone in his eyes whenever he looked at her. The fastest and easiest way to do that was to quash the beginning sparks of his attraction before they had the chance to grow into something truly dangerous.

He leaned toward her again, apparently not even the slightest bit deterred. "I don't believe that."

She shrugged. "Believe it or don't. It's no skin off my nose."

"Why'd you come back to Charleston? Why now?"

"It felt the safest place for me," she answered honestly, even though she knew full well it would be the first place Alan searched for her when he realized she'd left Alabama. She'd just have to deal with that when they got to it.

Nolan leaned forward again; his eyes held a new intensity as he studied her. "Are you in danger?"

"Not any more than usual," she answered truthfully. "Anyway, I'm sorry I was rude to you. Please don't fire me. I'll be better, I swear."

"I'm not going to fire you, Harmony, and I'll stop pressuring you to go out with me, but I would really like to be your friend if you'll let me." He put his hand on hers so that her much smaller fingers disappeared beneath his palm. A warmth she couldn't deny spread from her hand all the way up her arm and into her heart.

"I guess I can live with that," she whispered, hoping that it would prove to be true.

CHAPTER 18

HARMONY

The week that followed turned out to be strangely sublime. Harmony worked each morning at O'Brien's, then spent the afternoons snuggling with Muffin and exchanging backstories with Virginia as the older woman taught her to work a pair of knitting needles.

She saw Pastor Adam and Abigail more days than not, and with all the folks who now regularly frequented her life, she was beginning to feel a strange sense of belonging. A warmth glowed inside of her at the thought, but fear still shook her to the core.

Alan could still come to find her.

Would still come to find her.

She would have to run again and leave all these good people behind.

Muffin would be all right. He could go back to the church, and maybe in her next town she could adopt a dog in need to be her permanent companion. Because, yes, despite her initial hesitation, the little yapper had grown on her.

She hated the thought of another human in bed with her and had not once let Alan sleep over when they were dating, even though he'd begged on many occasions and even tried to force himself on her once or twice, too. But having Muffin glued to her side throughout the night gave her a special feeling of comfort she'd never quite had before.

For all his craziness and all their years apart, Pastor Adam had known exactly what she needed when he paired her with the spirited Chihuahua. Maybe one day Harmony would take to carrying him with her in a fancy shoulder bag after all.

She felt safer when Muffin was near, too. For one thing, he had a way of barking at even the slightest unexpected sound from outdoors. That meant no one could sneak up and surprise her. And for another, she knew Muffin would always have her side and didn't even doubt he'd bite a few ankles if he sensed danger.

It was amazing what five pounds of love could do to transform one's state of mind, or more specifically, *her* state of mind.

Harmony tied off the final row of stitches on her newly finished handicraft and lifted it triumphantly for Mrs. Clementine to admire. "Ta da, my first scarf!" she cried, feeling really quite proud despite the crooked rows and loose knit of the garment.

"Oh, let me get a picture." The landlady grabbed her phone and Harmony posed happily with her creation. Yes, life seemed worryingly simple these past several days.

And every day another of her walls crumbled, the people who were near to her moving deeper and deeper into her heart. Was this what God wanted for her? Is that why He'd sent her migrating back to the Holy City? Or was she being foolish to believe that things could ever change for her, especially after so many years of hardship?

It was almost as if she'd stumbled onto a family of her own. If Pastor Adam was her stand-in father, then surely Mrs. Clementine would be her mother and Abigail a sister, even little Owen a nephew. Jolene had become a close friend. As to Nolan, well, she was still deciding where he belonged in her life. Big brother didn't seem like the right label given their mutual attraction, but she sure as sugar didn't think of him as a husband, potential or otherwise.

That would be the day!

After her experience with Alan, she doubted she'd ever be able to stomach the idea of marriage at all. He'd, of course, asked her many times to become his wife, and each time she'd declined. She'd known something was off between them, but she didn't know enough to figure out what, didn't know how a healthy relationship should actually look.

Matter of fact, she still didn't know. Maybe it wasn't all that important for her to figure out, though.

Maybe it was enough to keep living each day on its own like stitches in a row—loop enough together and you could make something truly beautiful.

"I have some patterns if you'd like to start a new project," Virginia said as she showed Harmony the burst of pictures she'd taken just then. "Or I could show you how to macramé, needlepoint, or quilt. You name it, and we'll do it."

"It's a little chilly outside these days," Harmony said after a moment's thought. "Could you teach me to knit a sweater for Muffin?"

Yes, she was only a few degrees away from crazy when it came to fondness for her new dog, and perhaps a few dozen loops or so away from having a strong base for her new life.

Just so long as her past didn't come calling, her future might turn out very bright indeed.

CHAPTER 19

HARMONY

Harmony was granted the following day off work. Well, more like Nolan had insisted she take at least one day's break each week and refused to argue the point. Luckily, the tips at O'Brien's were good and the people friendly. She'd already paid Virginia for an entire month's room and board and still had a bit of cash on hand for something fun to pass the time.

She started with a long, leisurely visit to the dog park, because Muffin deserved a treat on their day off together, too. After that, she swung by the craft store and picked out a new pair of knitting needles in her favorite color, a shiny metallic red, along with a few attractive skeins of yarn as a thank you to Virginia for all the lessons and for so generously sharing her stash.

In that same strip mall sat a salon called Beauty by Belle. Harmony had never been much for pampering or fussing over her appearance, but now that she thought of it, a change did seem long overdue. Alan had loved her long, dark wavy hair. It would be freeing to change it up, not to mention so much easier to get ready in the morning.

She pushed her way into the mostly empty salon where a tiny, jingling bell announced her arrival.

"Have a seat, shugs, and I'll be right with you!" someone called from the back.

Harmony plopped into the chair closest to the door and studied herself in the mirror. She'd worn her minimalist makeup the same way since high school and had never done anything trendy or daring with her hair. Yes, it was definitely time for a change—perhaps a radical one. At worst she wouldn't like it and would find herself stuck with an unpleasant change until her hair grew back with a vengeance. At best she'd be euphoric with the new look and less recognizable should Alan come searching for her.

Because even though a good bit of time had passed, she still didn't believe she was out of the woods yet. He'd turn up eventually and find a very different Harmony waiting for him. Maybe he'd stop being attracted to her, too.

If only she could be so lucky.

"What can I do for you today?" a red-headed woman who looked to be about Harmony's age asked as she came up behind her in the chair. She wore a brightly colored maxi dress in a light floral pattern and thick combat boots that had surely seen better days.

"Something totally different," Harmony announced with an excited bounce of her shoulders.

The stylist wrinkled her nose. "Are you sure? Cuz a lot of time women come up in here saying the same thing but then wind up complaining that it's *too* different. And I lose myself a customer. Name's Avery, by the way, Avery Hollis."

"I'm Harmony, and—yes—I am 100% sure. Can you make it the exact opposite of what it's like now? I can take it." She waited, praying the woman would not only agree but come up with something fabulous.

Avery walked a slow circle around Harmony, taking in all her angles. "So seeing as you're long, dark, and curly as a before, I'm guessing you might like short, straight, and blonde as an after? How much time have you got?"

"As much time as it takes," Harmony said, wiggling her butt in the chair with anticipation.

"Belle!" the stylist hollered toward the back of the

house, startling Harmony by her sudden switch in volume. "Can you whip up a batch of bleach for me?"

"Sure thing!" came the cheery response.

"First I'll do a quick cut," Avery explained, snapping her scissors playfully. "Then we'll bleach ya, dye ya, and finally, we'll finish you up with an angled bob. Good?"

"Great." Harmony could hardly wait. Maybe all the time she now spent creating pretty things with Virginia was starting to rub off on her a bit more than she'd realized.

Avery spun her chair in a full circle. Her eyes widened as she said, "All right. Looks like we're going to have ourselves some fun this afternoon. Now, seeing as we'll be here for quite some time, you may as well start with your life story. Make it good. I do so love being entertained while I work."

Harmony swallowed, coughed, then licked her lips to stall for time.

"Oh, honey! Relax! You don't have to tell me anything you don't want to. It's just a lot of people use this chair as if'n they're in a shrink's office. You won't believe the things folks will confide in me when I'm wielding these here scissors."

"Actually," Harmony said, coming up with an

idea she rather liked. "I'd much rather hear about you."

Avery crossed her arms and shifted her weight so that one hip jutted out to the side. "About me, huh? Well, whatcha want to know?"

Harmony shrugged. "Start at the beginning?"

The stylist put one hand on her hip and snipped the scissors animatedly in her other hand as she thought. It was only then Harmony noticed just how thin the other woman was. Her full collarbone jutted out from her chest like a cylinder had just been stuck on for good measure. She could also see the faint outlines of her uppermost ribs.

Avery caught Harmony staring and quickly turned toward the counter that held her supplies. "Is it a bit cold in here?" she asked as she extracted a lumpy cardigan from the bottom drawer and shoved her arms into it, clearly embarrassed by the exchange.

"Have you seen Josephine Hannah's newest movie yet?" Harmony asked with a smile, hoping the change of topic would set Avery back at ease.

"The one that takes place in Alaska, you mean?" The stylist took a deep breath and began to spritz her client's hair with a hot pink water bottle.

"That's the one. I haven't found the time just yet,

but I heard it's her best to date. They say she actually fell in love while filming it, you know."

"With that hunky fireman?" Avery set the water bottle down and took the first of many snips with her scissors.

"Yes, he's a real cutie. Isn't he?" Harmony said amicably, even though Josephine Hannah's newest flame was not even close to her type. She preferred tall, blonde, and pushy, but no way was she ever going to admit that aloud.

"He sure is, but have you seen the new actor who's playing opposite Jo-Han in her next film?"

The two women laughed and carried on as new acquaintances with shared interests do. Harmony suspected she wasn't the only one who preferred to keep the conversation light and easy. She said a silent prayer that everything was all right in Avery's world and that everything would stay right with hers.

Oh, and that they wouldn't run out of handsome celebrities to discuss before Harmony's new hairstyle was finished.

CHAPTER 20

PASTOR ADAM

That day I brought Cupcake to my office with me for a bit of added company. The poor pup had been particularly disheartened since our Muffin moved out on assignment, so Abigail and I both tried to show her some extra love when we could.

I had a couple appointments scheduled for newlywed counseling, but mostly a quiet day to tend to my devotions and prepare my next sermon. Mrs. Clementine came in for a short while to discuss numbers and bills and whatnot, but I told her—as I always do—that I'd much rather she take charge of that so I'd know it was in capable hands instead of my own fumbling fingers.

By four o'clock, I was getting ready to head on

home, but an unexpected visitor found me before I'd made any of the usual motions to leave. Cupcake stood ramrod straight and stared at the door, a low growl sounding from her throat.

"Oh, you, hush now," I told the Chihuahua as I nudged her gently with the side of my foot, then called to our guest, "C'mon in!"

A fashionable young woman strode in with sunny yellow locks cut short against her neck. It took me a good thirty seconds to realize I knew her. "Harmony?" I gasped and covered my mouth with my hand in an attempt to minimize the rudeness of my unplanned gesture.

"I changed my hair," she said with a small grin.

"I see that," was my reply. "It's quite becoming."

Truth was, I liked her hair better in its previous incarnation, but Harmony seemed lighter, happier with this change, which made me like it very well for the aforementioned reasons.

"Thank you," she mouthed without quite voicing the words aloud.

"How can I help you this afternoon?" I prompted. Folks like Harmony didn't just show up unannounced for no reason.

She glanced around my office, then, seeing Cupcake, stooped down to pick her up and shower her with kisses. Ha, I'd known there was a dog person hidden in there!

When that Chihuahua was acceptably covered in kisses, Harmony looked back up at me and said, "Seeing as my head feels tons lighter, I figured it might also be time to unburden my soul." She shrugged as if she hadn't just said something monumental, especially for her.

"If you're looking to confess, there's a nice Catholic church right down the street," I joked. "But if you're here to seek counsel, then I'm all ears."

"Actually, it's a bit of both." She sank onto the couch and Cupcake settled onto her lap, then flipped on her side to demand a belly rub.

"Go ahead when you're ready and I'll do my best to help in whatever way I can."

She smiled, frowned, smiled again. Clearly it wasn't easy for her to be here, and I appreciated that she had sought me out despite her reservations. "I want to tell you why I came back to Charleston," she began, and the words that followed sent a special blend of sadness and rage to my very core.

That poor, poor child…

CHAPTER 21

HARMONY

"I'm here to talk about Alan." Harmony kept her eyes glued to the dog in her lap as she spoke. That made it easier to tell the full details of what had happened to trigger her Charleston homecoming. "I just heard word for Jolene that he's back in town and looking for me. Figured that meant it was time someone knew the full story. In case…" Her voice cracked, and she paused, unable to finish voicing the horrible thought aloud.

"Go ahead," the pastor told her. "I'm a good listener."

She let out a slow, shaky breath. Might as well start from the beginning, or at least their reintroduction as adults.

"Well, at first being with him was really nice," she

told the pastor. "Like I'd finally found someone who understood what I'd been through and didn't judge me for it. It was freeing in a way, knowing he just got it without me having to say a word, that it wouldn't be a problem later."

Pastor Adam nodded and steepled his fingers in front of his face as he listened. His expression remained neutral, although Harmony was certain hers flashed a full range of emotions.

"He was the perfect boyfriend as long as I never did anything to upset him. That's why it took me so long to notice something was wrong." She paused and shook her head. There were no tears left to cry, not for Alan and certainly not for herself. "I remember thinking that I was so lucky, that I'd finally found a family and that Alan and I were it, that we'd be together forever. He was attentive, showered me with compliments, was generous with his time and what little money he had, but it seemed there was a darkness in him."

She shivered as she recalled the first time she'd watched as something change in his eyes. The love he always wore transformed into the brightest burning hatred she'd ever seen in anyone. "One night I went out with some friends after work. I hadn't called to let Alan know since he had plans himself that evening, but when I got home, he was standing by my open door, waiting, glaring out into the darkness. He'd busted in, said he was worried when I hadn't answered my phone, thought something was wrong, that he loved me so much and couldn't stand the thought of anything happening to me. I'd told him my phone died, apologized a million times, and then we moved on. Things were good again for another few weeks after that."

The Pastor leaned back in his chair and crossed his arms over his chest, staying quiet because she still had words pouring out of her. Now that she'd started this difficult conversation, she just couldn't bring herself to stop until she reached the very end.

"He started checking in more often, making sure I called him once in the afternoon and once in the evening, asking about even the minutest details of my day. I started to consider myself lucky again, chalked it up to him just having had a bad day that one time. We all have bad days, right?"

Pastor Adam frowned, but nodded his head all the same.

Harmony let out a sad laugh and shivered again. The little dog in her lap had fallen asleep to the sound of her voice and was now having a dream that spurred her to twitch his legs and make tiny, whimpering sounds.

She took a deep breath and continued. "When he asked me to move in with him, I can honestly say I considered it, but in the end, I decided I'd rather keep my promise to God about staying pure. He took it hard, and even though he tried to hide his dissatisfaction, I felt something shift between us again. Not even a week later he asked me to marry him. He wanted to drive off to city hall that very moment—no more waiting, not even for a day.

"I knew he thought he was sweeping me up in this big, romantic moment, but honestly, I was scared. It was like the connection between us had severed and he no longer understood what I wanted or how I felt. When I said no, he asked if I was breaking up with him. I said no to that, too.

"And he started crying big, fat tears like I'd never seen a man cry before. He said if he lost me, he'd go crazy. He wouldn't know what to do. Maybe he would just kill himself now, he said, to save us both the trouble. I convinced him to stop crying, stop saying those horrible things. Told him I loved him, held him for a long time."

Pastor Adam sucked air in through his teeth, suggesting he knew exactly what was coming next.

And so she continued. "The next day he was obscenely happy, happier than I'd ever seen him. He'd brought over takeout from our favorite Chinese place, and we sat together on the couch to eat it and watch reruns on the cable TV. On a commercial break, he turned to me and said he'd given it a lot of thought... mind you, it had been less than twenty-four hours since our altercation the night before. He'd given it lots of thought, he said, and we didn't need a piece of paper in order to be married. We were already married in our hearts and we belonged to each other, and then he kissed me. He wouldn't stop. He pushed farther and farther, way past anything we'd ever done before, covered my body with his, and I could feel..."

Her voice cracked. "I could feel what he had planned, and it wasn't what I wanted. Not one bit. He kept coming at me even when I begged him to stop, and so I bit him. Hard. I bit him so hard, his lip was just spewing blood, and he called me awful names, then threw me off the couch so hard that the glass coffee table shattered from the force of me slamming into it. I ran and locked myself in the bathroom, begging him to go away.

"The next morning, my landlord stopped by, told me there had been too many complaints from the other tenants and I had until the end of the day to pack my things and move on. Alan didn't come round that day, I have no idea why. He called and seemed fine. We made plans to meet the next day because I figured that would keep him away long enough for me to get gone without him having to know where.

"He called at midnight to say he loved me. I didn't let him know that I had slept on a coworker's couch, that I had tossed most of my earthly possessions in a dumpster outside my old building. And the next day I woke up before the sun, grabbed my backpack, and left for Charleston."

She paused. Her shaky eyes locked onto his as she revealed, "The next person I spoke to was you."

CHAPTER 22

HARMONY

Harmony felt better now that someone else knew about what she'd been through with Alan, along with the disturbing fact that it likely wasn't over yet. Pastor Adam re-extended his offer for regular counseling and also suggested she go to the police, said he had a good friend in law enforcement who could keep an eye out for trouble.

She told him she'd consider both offers, thanked him for listening, and headed home to Virginia's. Along the way she wondered if she should try to purchase a gun to defend herself from the inevitable. She even went so far as to pull into the lot outside the tiny shack-like building that sold firearms and ammunition.

But no, she couldn't.

As much as she didn't want to die, she'd much rather Alan kill her than have to live with the knowledge that she'd willingly chosen to end someone else's life. Even if it was self-defense and she was thus never punished for taking action, her mind would still slowly deteriorate. Ultimately, she'd go mad with the guilt.

And that wasn't a price she was willing to pay.

Not even to guarantee her own safety.

She'd need to rely on her own wits, watchfulness, and a tiny Chihuahua who would do anything to keep her safe. Thankfully, God was always with her, too.

At home, she found Nolan and Pancake sitting on the front porch waiting for her return.

"Jolene told me everything!" he said, rushing forth to give her a tight hug. "Why didn't you tell me you were in danger?"

She pushed back from his chest, trying to ignore how good it felt to be wrapped in his strong embrace, to have someone who cared. "What makes you think I'm in danger?"

"Well, for starters, you're shaking like a leaf. Also, Jolene has her way of getting a good read on people. She said that the man who came for you was on the search for no good." His normally cheerful face twisted with rage. It figured he'd heard the news as well. Jolene told everything to everybody, but at least she'd kept mum when it came to Alan's request for information.

"Did you get his name?" she asked, unable to deny her fear anymore.

Nolan shook his head and swore under his breath. "No, he wouldn't give it. Jolene said he was just under six foot tall with dark hair and eyes. He was wearing track pants and a concert shirt but she couldn't remember the band."

"Sounds like Alan to a T. No one else would be looking for me besides him."

"What does he want?" Nolan placed a hand on her arm. He was shaking, too.

"I don't know. Revenge on me for leaving him? Or, maybe just the opposite, that he wants to convince me to give him another try." Harmony sucked air through her teeth, but it wasn't enough to steady her or calm Nolan.

"You've got to be kidding me." He ran both hands through his hair and kicked at the pavement leading up to Mrs. Clementine's wrap-around porch.

"I wouldn't kid about something like this," she shot back. "I left and got as far as I could as quick as I could for a reason."

"Did he hurt you? Before you left? Was he…?" Nolan shook with rage so much so that she now felt the need to place a calming hand on his arm.

"Yes," Harmony told him. "Yes, he did hurt me, and I'm pretty sure he'd do it again if he got the chance. I'm not sure he meant to but—"

"But nothing!" Nolan exploded, causing Harmony to take a step back. "It's never okay. Never."

Pancake stood to his full height and let out a low growl. Inside the house, Muffin barked manically, begging to be let out to join whatever fight was unfolding.

"I have to get him before he goes nuts," she said to Nolan. "Try to calm down some. I don't want Muffin thinking he has to protect me from you."

The little dog squeezed through the doorway before Harmony could even open the door wider than a few inches. Once outside, he raced in a big loop, searching for the source of the agitation. When he deemed Nolan and Pancake to be of no danger, he trotted back to Harmony and stood on his hind legs, asking to be picked up.

"It's okay, Muffs." She scratched the little dog between his ears. He looked so proud of his guard-dogging efforts that she couldn't help but smile.

"I won't let him hurt you," Nolan said in a flat, eerie voice. "If I have to stakeout this place every night just to make sure you're safe, I will."

She blinked hard. "What are you going to do, Nolan? Park your car down the street and watch for suspicious characters?"

"If that's what it takes." He crossed his arms, and the gesture made him seem impossibly large, just like his oversized dog.

"Look, I appreciate the support, I do. But why don't you just come inside for a bit to calm down? Virginia usually has supper on the table by now, and I'm sure she'd be happy to have you join us."

He let out a frustrated sigh. "But Harmony—"

"But nothing. I've survived all these twenty-seven years. Surely I can survive the night. Unless you're saying I'm not strong enough to look after myself."

"It's not that."

"Then what is it?"

He took a deep breath, then let his shoulders fall. A moment later, he pulled out a small smile and said, "What do you suppose Mrs. Clementine has cooked tonight?"

"Let's go find out." Harmony opened the door and waited for him and Pancake to pass inside, then took one last look toward the street. When she saw that no strange or familiar cars idled nearby, she shut the door firmly behind her and, with it, her fears.

She could let Alan rule every second of her world the way he wanted to, or she could push her worry deep down and try to get on with her life.

For now, she chose the latter.

CHAPTER 23

HARMONY

Harmony leaned forward to whisper into Nolan's ear—actually, given their height difference, it was more like his shoulder. "Not a word of this to Virginia. I'd hate for her to worry."

"But—"

She jabbed her finger into his chest hard, which cut that argument off at the quick, then shook the same finger in front of his face and warned, "Not. A. Word."

"Have it your way," he said, kicking off his shoes in a defeated gesture, then lining them up neatly side-by-side in the coat closet. "But seeing as I already know and I'm already worried, I hope you can tell me more later."

"Fine," she agreed. "But later."

"Virginia," Harmony called as they headed toward the kitchen with both dogs trailing behind. "We have visitors!"

They found her standing in front of a fry pan tending to a simmering batch of greens that had been smothered to within an inch of their life with butter.

"Smells great," Nolan said, taking a long, appreciative sniff of the air that hung heavy in the kitchen. "Thanks for having me and Pancake. That is, if you'll have us. I didn't exactly hear Harmony ask."

Harmony's jaw fell open. Now he was lecturing her on proper decorum? Of all the teachers in the world, he hardly seemed the most qualified in this particular subject.

Mrs. Clementine, however, was in her element. "Of course!" the old woman crooned. "The more, the merrier. I always make too much and end up bringing the leftovers to Pastor Elliott the day after. I'm afraid it's starting to show on his waistline. You, however, look like you have plenty of room to expand on that tall frame of yours."

Harmony laughed as she pictured Nolan with a spare tire to match the pastor's, and it softened her feelings toward him once again. Still, she hoped the lack of leftovers wouldn't disappoint Pastor Adam too much, especially after the conversation they'd had earlier that evening.

"What are we having tonight?" she asked. "And how can I help?"

Virginia shook the pan then settled it back on the burner. "Just a chicken and rice casserole. I realized afterward that I forgot to include even an ounce of vegetables, so I busted out the turnip greens to right that situation. Harmony, would you please go ahead and pour the tea?"

Ten minutes later, they were settled around the table with the delicious spread before them.

"I must confess," Ginny said as she glanced from her plate to Nolan. "I'm a bit nervous for a professional like yourself to be tasting my food. If I'd known in advance that you'd be gracing us with your company I'd have whipped out *The Joy of Cooking*. Maybe tried one of those fancy French recipes."

"Oh, please. I scramble eggs and flip flapjacks. This—" He paused to load up his fork with a heaping bite that contained a little of everything. "—Is much more impressive." He even made a series of loud, appreciative sounds to prove his point.

Both dogs whined and shook their fluffy butts but stayed sitting where Harmony had instructed for them to wait.

"I'm glad it meets your approval." Virginia noticeably relaxed now that she had Nolan's good opinion. "Now, to what do we owe the pleasure?"

Harmony kicked him under the table to remind him of their deal.

"Oh, ouch, um…" Nolan, who was terrible at being subtle, swallowed his bite, took a sip of sweet tea, and then started over. "I came by to ask Harmony on a date, and she invited me in for your famous home cooking instead."

"Oh, Harmony," her landlady said with a sigh. "While I do appreciate the company, you'll have a much more enjoyable courtship without me tagging along as your third wheel."

"Point taken," Harmony said peaceably, wracking her brain for a change of topic.

But before she could come up with something satisfactory, Ginny spoke again. "You two do make such a nice couple. I could see the chemistry between you right away. Look, even your dogs are just smitten with each other."

Everyone glanced toward Muffin and Pancake. The two of whom had decided to lay down and cuddle up in each other's warmth as they watched for any stray bit of food that might be dropped from the table.

"They sure are," Nolan said, and then everyone laughed as both dogs tilted their heads in the same direction, almost like a synchronized dance—never mind that the little dog's entire body was still smaller than just the great Wolfhound's head.

"Love is funny like that," Virginia said. "If you'd told me all those years ago that I'd wind up married to Mr. Clementine, I'd have argued with you until I was blue in the face. Yet here we are, more than thirty years later, and still just as happy as the day we said 'I do.'"

Harmony smiled and nodded. In all the time she had been living with Virginia, she had not even met the man once, and he'd only called to talk to his wife a handful of times. While she loved Mrs. Clementine dearly, Harmony often asked herself whether her new friend was in denial or simply trying her best to hide her collapsing marriage from others. Harmony did what she could by praying for them each and every night.

If their relationship, however, showed what happily married looked like, then she was definitely better off alone.

CHAPTER 24

HARMONY

The next day started to feel normal again despite the scare Alan's appearance had been given to everyone. Jolene, of course, rushed to tell her version of the run-in with Harmony's ex, but Nolan mostly hung back in the kitchen and focused on his work. Once they'd finished their closing duties, he offered to escort Harmony back to Virginia's house.

"I kind of have my own car," she told him with a forced laugh.

"I'll follow you. C'mon." He checked and double-checked that the restaurant was locked up tight, then walked with her to the parking lot where they'd left both their cars that morning.

"I appreciate what you're trying to do for me, but really, it's not necessary."

"Who says I'm doing this for you? I'll worry about you the whole rest of the day if I don't see for myself that you get home safely."

Harmony fought back the fear that began to settle in her gut. It had been like this with Alan once, too. He'd wanted to be with her all the time, go everywhere she went, and called to check in frequently whenever they were apart. At first she'd thought it was because he loved her so much. Sadly, by the time she realized that it was all about controlling her, she was already too deeply involved.

Nolan had been nothing but kind to her. But still…

Could history repeat itself, turning him into either his mean sister or her crazy ex? She hated that everything set her on edge, that she couldn't simply trust and enjoy her budding friendship with the nice man, but in the past, everyone had always let her down.

Why would Nolan be any different?

Even people who seemed nice in the start could still disappoint you. In fact, they were often the ones who wound up hurting you worst of anybody. It only made sense to keep the walls up around her heart and her life. If Nolan wanted to see her home, fine…but she wouldn't let him in. She wouldn't let him use her potentially dangerous ex as an excuse to get his hooks into her just as deep as Alan's had once been.

"You can see me home," she told him, stopping at her car door without getting in. "But you can't come in. Not today."

He nodded and broke into a smile as if she were the one doing him a favor in this situation. "That's perfect. I've got my basketball league this afternoon anyway. No extra time for visiting." Figured he played basketball. He was probably the best player on the team, too. Few men around these parts came within an inch of his great height.

She eyed him suspiciously. Was he merely telling her what he thought she wanted to hear, or did he truly only care about making sure she was safe?

"Look," he said, tossing his keys up in the air and then catching him in his opposite fist deftly. "I know you've been through some awful stuff. I also know enough to know that I don't know the half of it."

He laughed at his jumbled turn of phrase. "The point is, I promised to be your friend, and as part of that, I want you to know that you can trust me."

"I do trust you," she argued, knowing even as she spoke the words that they weren't true. It was nothing against Nolan—she simply preferred not to trust *anyone*. It was the surest way to make sure she didn't get hurt again.

"You're getting there," he said. "But I can see that you need more time. You shouldn't just blindly trust people. You're right about that, but I'm also right when I say that I'm going to earn your trust fair and square."

She couldn't help but admire his determination. It was well matched to her stubbornness. "We'll see about that," she said with a poorly disguised grin.

"Oh, we will." He winked at her, and she wasn't sure why. "For starters, I want you to know that our talk the other day didn't fall on deaf ears. I had it out with my sister."

This surprised her. What could Nolan possibly have to gain by confronting Megan? How would it help anything?

"She remembers putting you through hell and says she's very sorry."

Harmony let out a sarcastic laugh. She just couldn't help it.

"I know. Likely story, right? Except she did seem genuinely apologetic, and she even asked if she could meet with you in person to say sorry."

Static pricked at the hairs on Harmony's arms.

"Nolan! You didn't invite her to the restaurant, did you?"

"No, I wouldn't do that. She doesn't even know you're working here. I told her I'd ask you along to the Eternal Grace Church picnic later this month, and if you agreed she could apologize then and there. Gives you some time to think and prepare. Although I do hope you'll say yes."

"Yes," Harmony said without hesitation.

His eyes lit up and a smile began to creep from one cheek to the other.

"Yes, I'll think about it," she clarified. "Not yes I'll go. That has yet to be determined."

"Fair enough," he said, slapping his hand on the hood of her car and then bending forward to open her driver's side door. "Now let's get you home. If we stand here chit-chatting any longer, I'm afraid I'll be late for my practice."

Harmony reached up and gave him a quick hug. "Thank you for being my friend," she said. "I know it's not easy, but I'm glad you're up for the challenge."

Nolan cleared his throat and squeezed her tight. "I sure am," he agreed. "I sure am."

CHAPTER 25

PASTOR ADAM

Our spring potluck arrived just as the daffodils that lined the church flowerbeds had begun to unfurl their happy yellow petals to greet the season. Mrs. Clementine had planted them as one of her first acts when she took up the role as church secretary, and every season I was grateful to see them, seeing as they heralded warmer weather as well as the anniversary of our Lord and Savior's resurrection.

Last autumn she'd elected to remove the vegetable patch in favor of more flowers, and to say I was grateful would be an understatement of biblical proportions. I much preferred the pretty tulips that had taken the cucumbers' and tomatoes' places, and we had far fewer critters who showed up to wreak havoc on the brightly colored flowers.

Our church yard wasn't enormous, but we still insisted on having a picnic there at the change of each season and invited not just our whole congregation, but the entire town of Charleston.

Some folks came to eat and run, and that was just fine by me. Others lingered inside, while the more adventurous set up blankets outdoors where they could enjoy our newly awakened gardens.

This was to be my grandson's first spring potluck, seeing as he was born at the end of the season the year prior. He'd be walking any day now, too. Gavin and Abigail were all too proud to show him off to the folks that were ECP churchgoers—that's Easter, Christmas, Potluck—and they all gushed and gushed over his cuteness.

Rightfully so, I might add.

Yes, Gavin and Abigail made quite the beautiful couple. It wasn't just their faces that looked good together, but their hearts matched, too. Hallelujah, the Lord is good!

Mama Mary stayed glued to Abigail's side as she always did, but the younger church dogs roamed freely about the lot to greet our guests and beg for scraps.

We placed several signs around the yard reminding folks not to feed the Chihuahuas but still, I suspect their tummies ended up full and well fed all the same.

One of the dogs bounded up to me and began to whine and scratch at my shins. It took me a moment to realize it was our working-on-location church dog, Muffin. Which meant...

"Harmony!" I cried the moment I saw her and stretched my arms wide to saddle her with a hug. I'd had a few weeks to get accustomed to her new hairstyle now, and it had grown on me. "I'm so happy you came."

"Well, you can thank this guy," she said with a half-smile, bumping her shoulder into Nolan Murphy's arm.

I turned to the tall chap and offered him a smile since his hands appeared to full to join me in a shake. "Nolan, it's good to see you, too."

"I brought some grits and sausage for the spread," he said, lifting up a crock pot that he'd carried over with him.

"Tables are over there under the tent," I instructed.

Nolan nodded and headed off decisively in the direction I had pointed while Harmony remained back standing beside me.

"I thought about your offer for counseling some more," she said, dropping her voice so quiet I could hardly hear her. "I'd like to do it, provided the offer still stands."

I took her hand in both of mine and gave it a good, firm shake. "See you Tuesday."

She agreed and then skipped off to join Nolan by the food.

Okay, so she didn't skip, but she didn't sulk, either. There was a certain peppiness to her step that hadn't been there before, and seeing as I'd been in love once before myself and had counseled countless others on the merits of 1 Corinthians 13, I knew exactly what had gotten into Miss Harmony King.

That Nolan was good for her.

And even if she hadn't realized it yet, I had no doubts. And so I made sure to mentally leave a section of my schedule open for their inevitable premarital counseling.

CHAPTER 26

HARMONY

Harmony let Nolan hold her hand as he guided her toward his sister.

Megan, who was setting up a store-bought veggie tray on the far end of the food tent, smiled as she spotted the two of them heading her way.

"Harmony," she cried. A look of anguish washed over her face, making her otherwise pretty features appear mangled. "I'm so glad you agreed to come!"

"Hello, Megan," she said, tucking her short, blonde hair behind her ears on both sides. Truth be told, she'd almost backed out of the whole affair. What good would seeing her former bully do for her now that she had a far more threatening figure stalking the outer edges of her life?

Alan hadn't shown himself again, at least not that she'd seen or heard. Still, Nolan insisted on escorting her home after each and every shift. He waited in the parking lot for her arrival in the mornings as well. True to his word, he never pushed Harmony for more of an explanation about her past or for more of a relationship than she could handle, putting her initial worries aside.

Now the biggest lingering concern was why Alan hadn't found her yet. Could he have really given up so quickly? It seemed unlikely, and yet as each day passed, Harmony began to feel more and more at ease in her new life.

Now's not the time for this. She willed her thoughts to be silent and focused her attention on Megan, who stood waiting before her with an expectant, awkward smile.

"Should we get some food before we catch up?" Nolan's sister asked. Like her brother, she had light blonde hair and freckles. Unlike him, however, Megan's good looks seemed to have peaked in high school. She was still attractive enough, especially when she smiled, but was nowhere near the knockout she'd once been.

Still, Harmony found herself envying the woman's tall, slender frame and ample chest. She'd been among the first of the girls at their school to bloom into a woman, while Harmony had been one of the last. Thinking about it now, Harmony felt that familiar old surge of jealousy swell.

"I'm not too hungry," she said waving a hand dismissively. The last thing she needed was to throw up church food on her former bully—no matter how funny it might be to revisit that moment later. "Could we talk first and grab food a bit later?"

"Sure, okay." Megan led them away from the food tent and toward a blanket she'd set up near the edge of the daffodils.

Harmony sat first, and Nolan sank down beside her, sitting close enough to lend his warmth without the two of them actually having to touch.

Megan swayed back and forth before finally lowering herself to her knees and then leaning back on her heels. That tormented look was back, and Harmony wondered if Megan had ever thought about her at all between high school graduation and Nolan's mention of her earlier that month.

Focusing her gaze on Harmony, she frowned and said, "I really, truly am so sorry for how I treated you during our school days. I'm just torn up about it."

Sure you are, Harmony thought bitterly. She'd long since stopped dwelling on the bad things Megan had done to her back then, but it didn't make facing the woman now any easier.

"I was going through some rough stuff back then. Not that it excuses how I behaved but…" She licked her lips and looked away.

Going through stuff for more than six years? That's a lot of stuff. Harmony thought the words on the inside but managed to plaster on a smile on the outside.

"It's okay," Harmony told her. "I understand and I'm not angry anymore."

Megan breathed a huge sigh of relief and then settled into a more comfortable position. "Really? Do you mean it?"

"I do," Harmony said with a nod.

Nolan reached over and squeezed her hand.

"I forgive you," she said.

"Oh, Harmony!" Suddenly Megan had hurled herself across the blanket and now had Harmony wrapped in a rather uncomfortable hug. "You have no idea what a relief that is to hear. I really am so, so sorry and hope we can start over. Can we?"

"Sure," came her answer.

Nolan moved to let go of her hand but she hung on tight. While it was nice that his sister had apologized and clearly she felt better about it, Harmony felt just the same as she always had.

Sorry didn't erase all the tears that had already been shed. Sometimes mistakes couldn't be reversed. The best anyone could do was to try to learn from them and then move on. It seemed that Megan at least had tried to do that, but it didn't make Harmony want to become best friends with her all of a sudden, either.

"Tell me about you," Megan said. Her eyes sparkled in the same way her brother's often did. "How long have you been back in Charleston? Where are you staying?"

"Little over a month now, and I'm renting a room from Virginia Clementine."

"Oh, she's such a nice lady," Megan said, clasping her hands together as if Harmony was a puppy who'd just performed a cute trick right on cue. "What else? What did you do after we graduated? What are you doing now?"

Harmony took a deep breath and began her story, or at least the PG version with no curse words, no scary parts, and—most importantly—no bad guys.

CHAPTER 27

HARMONY

Harmony sat chatting politely with Megan for about an hour, but by then, she'd reached the limit for how much chitchat she could handle in one day without losing her temper. Nolan saw it, too.

"Hey," he said softly when Megan had turned to talk to a woman whom Harmony didn't recognize but that Megan appeared to know well. "Want to get out of here?"

She nodded, not even teasing him about the fact he'd used yet another bad pick-up line on her.

Nolan wasted no time rising to his feet and stretching his arms high overhead. A giant, theatrical yawn drew his sister's attention to him. "Welp. That's enough sun and socializing for one day," he announced. "Harmony, do you mind if we head out of here early? I'm sorry, but my Irish skin just can't take anymore without bursting into a punishing amount of freckles."

"Sure, seeing as you're my ride. Thanks for that, by the way." She stood now, too.

Megan smirked at her brother. "The Irishman in the sun excuse doesn't really work when you're with family," she pointed out. "But you and Harmony make a really cute couple, so I'm cool with it."

They both accepted hugs from Nolan's sister. Neither corrected her about the status of their couple-hood, which meant their escape was swift.

"Thanks again," she told him once they were safely settled in his car. "I don't think I could have lasted much longer."

"You betcha. Coming at all took some serious guts," he agreed with a nod while keeping his eyes focused on the road ahead. "Add it to the long list of things I really like about you."

She rolled her eyes. "Whatever you say."

"Where to now, Madame?" He adjusted both hands on the wheel and sat straighter in his seat, the very portrait of a proper chauffer. It was adorable, but still, Harmony was very tired.

"Home?" She looked down at Muffin, who sat

proudly on her lap with his tongue lolling out the side of his mouth. He didn't seem ready to call it a day, even though the short outing had exhausted Harmony.

"Nope, I'm not letting you off the hook that easy. You promised we'd spend the potluck together, and that thing is nowhere close to over."

Muffin barked in agreement, then stood with his front legs against the door and scratched at the window until Harmony relented and rolled it down for him.

"So you're taking me hostage?" she asked with one eyebrow quirked.

"Only until..." He glanced at his car's dash to get the time. "Four o'clock?"

"I guess that's fair. What would you like to do?"

"I have the perfect plan, but first we need to swing by and pick up Pancake. It wouldn't be fair to let Muffin have all the fun when he's stuck at home."

At the mention of his name, the fawn-colored Chihuahua popped down from his perch at the window and scurried over to Nolan's lap.

Harmony had to grab the little dog quickly so as not to interfere with his driving. "We headed to the dog park?" she asked with a laugh. "That sounds fun and is clearly needed."

He smiled. "Nope, it's even better than that. And nope, I'm not going to tell before we get there."

Harmony crossed her arms over her chest in mock outrage. "Don't I even get a hint?"

"A hint? Hmmm." He thought for a moment, even going so far as to scratch his chin like an old-fashioned detective.

She couldn't help but laugh. Spending time with Nolan was becoming easier by the day. In fact, she could honestly say it had become her favorite part of most days. She was so glad that she'd agreed to be friends and that he hadn't pushed her for more that she could offer.

Nolan stopped for a traffic light, then turned toward Harmony in his seat. "Here's your hint: it was one of my favorite places as a kid. And a teen. And now, actually."

Harmony groaned. "But, Mr. Murphy, sir, I don't want to go into work on my day off!"

"*Ha ha,*" he said pointedly, even going so far as to stick out his tongue at her. "This place is way cooler than O'Brien's, but don't tell anyone—and I mean *anyone*—I said that."

"Okay, what makes you like it so much, then? Expand the hint, please."

The light shifted back to green, and Nolan let out

a dreamy sigh as he turned his attention back to the road. "It's funny, I loved it as a kid because of all the excitement. Now I love it because of the calm. Strange how the same place can represent two very different things even to the same person, isn't it?"

She nodded. That was exactly how she felt about the whole of Charleston. On the one hand, it was the site of her unhappy childhood, while on the other, she was building a life she rather liked here now.

"Add to that the fact dogs are clearly allowed if we're going to pick up Pancake, and I still don't have enough to go on," she said thoughtfully. "You're going to have to give me more."

He considered this for a moment before agreeing. "Okay. How about I share my favorite memory of that place, then?"

"I'd love to hear it, especially if it's going to give me clues. Have I told you how much I don't like surprises?" Surprises for a foster kid were almost never of the welcome variety, and Harmony had continued her disdain for them with her into adulthood.

A smile crept across his face as he adjusted his hands on the steering wheel once more. "I promise you'll like this one. In fact, I think it's just what you need after the day you've had. Have I mentioned how gutsy I think you are for meeting with Megan?"

She groaned again. "Okay, on with the story, please."

"It's one of my earliest memories actually. For years, we hosted the Murphy-O'Brien family reunions there. My cousins would fly in from all over the country, and it was usually the only time we saw each other for the entire year. Being little boys, we each tried to prove how tough we were. Mind you, none of us were as tough as you."

Harmony laughed at this particular assertion but enjoyed his story all the same.

"It was great fun. We made weapons out of sticks and chased each other around all day, then at night, just before the sun went down, our dads sent us to find driftwood along the shore. We, of course, had a competition to see who could collect the most. I was so proud when I realized I'd won, but what was even better was the massive bonfire that we built after. We sat on the sand watching the flames stretch to the sky, and then we roasted hotdogs and marshmallows and had ourselves a right feast. I fell asleep staring into that fire and begged to make another every year that followed."

Harmony closed her eyes and pictured the scene as Nolan had described it. Even though he'd tried to be secretive, words like driftwood and shore gave his location away all the same. "Did you?" she asked, imagining the tall pyre reaching for the sky.

He chuckled sadly and shook his head. "No, apparently, our parents had unknowingly broken the law and were slapped with a heavy fine. I'm still grateful for the one bonfire we managed, though. To me, it was priceless."

"That's a beautiful memory, but you know you sound like a MasterCard commercial, right?" Harmony reached over and put a hand on his shoulder.

And he brought up his hand to rest on top of hers, almost as if he were keeping it captive, as if he never wanted her to let go. "Fair enough. And if you were paying attention, then you already know where we're going."

Sure enough, they arrived about twenty minutes later with both dogs in tow. The beach had never looked quite so beautiful to Harmony as it did that day.

CHAPTER 28

HARMONY

Harmony and Nolan took off their shoes, rolled up their pants, and strolled through the chilly surf. Seeing as most folks were still at the church potluck or else waiting for a warmer day to visit the beach, they mostly had the place to themselves.

Well, them and the two wildly happy dogs who ran big, looping circles around them as they progressed along the shoreline.

"You're right about it being peaceful," Harmony said. Even the shock of the cold ocean water between her toes felt like an important part of the experience. All they needed now was a bit of moonlight for the perfect romantic moment. Only... she'd taken romance completely off the table, and despite occasional moments of longing like the one she was facing now, Harmony knew she'd been right to do so.

Nolan remained thoughtful as their heels pressed down into the wet sand, leaving uneven tracks behind them.

"Thank you for sharing your memory about the bonfire. It's almost like I was right there with you."

"It would have been a very different kind of memory had you been there," he answered with a nostalgic grin. "Probably even better."

Harmony chuckled and reached for his hand, then caught herself and pulled back again. "Would you believe I've never been to a bonfire?"

Nolan stopped walking and regarded her suspiciously. "Never?"

She shook her head and giggled. "Nope, no campfires, either."

"What?" he practically shouted. "Why the heck not?"

"One of the joys of being a foster kid. None of our temporary guardians were too concerned about making memories with us."

His face fell, and before she knew it, he'd pulled her to his chest in a hug.

She laughed nervously against him but didn't push away. "Nolan. Really, it's okay."

Nolan stroked her hair and made calming noises as if she were the one who was upset and needed to be calmed. He clucked his tongue and mumbled half to himself, "If you've never had a fire, I'm guessing you've also never had s'mores, and that will not do."

"I know what s'mores are," she countered, leaning back to glare into his eyes. "And I doubt I'm so deprived that it warrants all these theatrics."

He squeezed her close again. "You're wrong about that, and we're going to fix it. We're going to fix it tonight."

"Nolan, really, it's fine."

"It isn't yet, but it will be soon." He released her, then turned back and started walking in the direction from which they'd first come.

The dogs spotted the sudden shift and chased after him, barking merrily as they pushed through the gentle waves. Pancake stopped often to make sure his little buddy was still with him, making Harmony's heart swell with love for both creatures.

She followed after man and dogs, moving in double time to catch up with Nolan's long, determined stride. "I'm having a nice time at the beach. Can't s'mores wait?"

He kept moving at his impossibly quick pace without even looking back. "Spoken like someone who's never tried the little pieces of heaven," he called over the sound of gulls crying and waves lapping at the shore. "Yes, we'll definitely need to fix that."

Harmony laughed and shook her head, even though secretly she was quite flattered that Nolan wanted her to experience all of his favorite memories. It was almost as if she were making up for all the time lost during her childhood. Getting a second chance to do things right.

"Okay, so what now?" she asked when the car loomed back into view.

"I'm going to drop you off at home, head to the store to grab some supplies, and then come back to introduce you to the best dessert this world has to offer. Hey, do you know if Mrs. Clementine has a fire pit?" He grabbed his keys from his pocket and unlocked the car. Its lights flashed in greetings.

Harmony's legs had begun to ache from the sudden burst of exercise, but luckily it was nearing its natural end. "I don't know, but I can ask," she said. "And why can't I come with you to get supplies? It's not like the recipe is a secret."

He turned to her for a moment, mischief flashing in his green eyes. "No, but I have a surprise for you nonetheless."

"*Nonetheless?* Who says nonetheless? And what did I tell you about surprises?"

"Trust me, it will be worth it."

It was then Harmony realized that she *did* trust him. Not just a little, not just partially, but all the way. She wasn't sure when the shift had occurred or what it meant for the future of their friendship—or her job, for that matter—but she'd have to unpack that later.

Right now, they had urgent s'mores business to attend to.

CHAPTER 29

HARMONY

The sun had already begun to set by the time Nolan and Pancake returned to Mrs. Clementine's house. Sure enough, Virginia had an old fire pit buried in her garden shed that she allowed Harmony to dig out for use in their so-called s'mores emergency.

She fitted Muffin's newly knit sweater onto his tiny, shivering body, knowing the night air would be too cold for him without the added layer of fuzz. And, really, she was quite proud of her handiwork. She'd alternated two skeins of yarn to create adorable blue and yellow stripes. Virginia had even helped her out by making a tiny hat to go with it. Now Muffin looked too cute for words in this new ensemble, although he seemed to believe his hat made a better chew toy than fashion accessory.

"Sorry it took me so long!" Nolan cried, setting a few very full grocery bags on the countertop.

Pancake, whose massive head reached over the counter without any added stretching on his part, sniffed determinedly at the corner of one of the bags.

His owner pushed the dog aside with his hip. "First Harmony, then you!" he told the Irish Wolfhound.

"I thought dogs couldn't have chocolate," Harmony reminded him gently. In fact, she was sure of it. Abigail's church dog manual had been very clear on the point—no chocolate, raisins, onions, and about a dozen other things as well.

"They can't." Nolan drew what looked like a camouflaged fishing pole out from a bag and began to crank its handle. The little metal prongs on the end spun slowly in what had to be the most ridiculous roasting stick in the entire world.

"That's why they're having sausages while we have the good stuff. Wouldn't want to leave the puppers out of this important memory," Nolan continued, handing her the camo stick rod hybrid thing, then pulling a second matching one from the bag.

There were still two and a half full grocery bags on the counter.

"How much do you expect us to eat?" Harmony asked, tossing a glance at the unnecessarily exorbitant amount of supplies.

"At least three s'mores each," he answered with a smile. "Since this is your first time, you need to have the classic, the alternate, and the original. That makes three." He put up three fingers as if this somehow further confirmed his assertion.

"I had no idea it was so involved." She nodded then broke apart in giggles. Leave it to Nolan to turn everything into a production.

"Well, obviously, that's why I'm here to teach you!"

"Obviously," she said, unable to hide her excitement and unwilling to even try. Nolan's enthusiasm was infectious, and she was eating it right up.

After a bit more rummaging, he grabbed the bags and headed for the sliding glass door.

Harmony rushed forward to open it for him and, in short order, they had a modest fire flickering before them. Virginia had also lent them two folded camping chairs to use for this backyard adventure. It seemed that woman was prepared for any eventuality, and Harmony felt grateful for it and to her.

She sat now with her knees pressed together and the roast stick dangling loosely from one hand.

"Are you ready?" Nolan's eyes shone brighter than the fire. She wondered if this whole thing was providing him with the chance to relive one of his favorite firsts as well.

She nodded and pointed her stick toward the sky. "Marshmallow me up, baby."

And although Harmony was very careful with how she positioned her stick, her marshmallow broke into flames almost immediately after setting it near the fire.

"Whoa!" Nolan cried, blowing it out for her and unwrapping a package of graham crackers as quickly as his fingers would allow. "That's okay! The burnt bits add flavor," he told her as he pressed a graham cracker square on either side of the marshmallow and pulled it off her stick.

Harmony unwrapped the waiting Hershey bar, added a slab of chocolate, and then took a giant, appreciative bite. "How can something so simple be so wonderful?" she mumbled around her very large, very delicious mouthful.

"That's the beauty of the s'mores, and of life, too," he said with a goofy grin. "Okay, so you've had the classic. Now you need to have the alternate. The only difference is that you make it with a peanut butter cup instead of pure chocolate."

"Sign me up for one of those," she said eagerly, relieved she'd chosen not to eat much at the potluck since she now planned to dine on s'mores until her stomach couldn't take it anymore.

The alternate s'mores were just as delicious as the originals. Harmony was glad Nolan had decided that making desserts over the fire would be the perfect way to end their special day together. This was one first she regretted not having much, much earlier in life.

"Ready for the original? It's my own recipe that I just developed today, actually." He looked so excited she could hardly stand it. Had he always been this adorable, or did her newfound trust add an extra layer of attraction that hadn't been there before?

"Ooh," she gushed, enjoying herself immensely. "What's in it? If it's as good as the others, then I'm in."

"It's definitely just as good," Nolan promised. "It's also totally different."

She pointed at him as if he'd just said something brilliant. "I guess that's why you call it the original."

"Actually, I call it the Harmony. The Harmony S'more." He kept his eyes fixed on her, awaiting the inevitable reaction.

"You named it after me?" She suddenly felt incredibly touched by the gesture, by this whole day she'd had with Nolan.

"I had to, seeing as you inspired it."

"How'd I do that?"

"Allow me to explain." He paused to add a marshmallow to each of their roasting sticks. "We start with the marshmallow, which is sweet, fun to look at, and also required to make this a s'more."

Harmony giggled. "And also liable to catch fire at a moment's notice, right?"

Nolan laughed, too. "Nope. For that, we have the gingersnap." He pulled out a Tupperware of what appeared to be homemade cookies. "Hard exterior, filled with interesting, unexpected flavors and—let's be honest here—also thoroughly Southern."

"I like where you're headed so far. What's next?"

"I'm glad you asked, because this is the best part." He brought a glass jar out from the bag followed in short order by a plastic butter knife. "Strawberry jam. Not what you'd expect to round out your s'mores, yet somehow it's perfect just the same. It also represents your guts."

"That's a little bit gross, but I like it all the same. Definitely a good description of me."

They both laughed as their marshmallows finished

roasting, and Nolan spread jam on a pair of ginger-snaps in preparation. When the full dessert was built, Harmony studied it a moment before taking a bite. "The Harmony S'more, huh?"

"The Harmony S'more," he echoed. "The perfect blend of spicy and sweet. Just like you."

Their eyes locked and neither said anything until a bit of hot marshmallow goop oozed onto Harmony's finger, bringing her focus back to the morsel before her.

She took a big bite and silently prayed that she wasn't about to go doing something so foolish as falling in love with Nolan Murphy.

CHAPTER 30

PASTOR ADAM

The church potluck last weekend was a smashing success, and I couldn't be happier. Even though its primary purpose was to offer fellowship among our members and the community at large, Eternal Grace still managed to raise enough money to fund our Resurrection Sunday stage play, complete with costumes, beautifully painted backdrops, and all the bells and whistles. I know the kids are beside themselves with excitement, and so am I.

Tonight my daughter, grandson, the church dogs, and I decided to enjoy a quiet night at home. My future son-in-law Gavin dropped by, too. Even though it will be much lonelier for me when Abigail and little Owen move out, I'm looking forward to officially welcoming this kind-hearted young man into the family.

He's a good man, made even better by the fact that he cooked supper for us tonight—and better than better for the fact that it was really quite tasty. I'm not too proud to admit that I helped myself to seconds and thirds of his pot roast stew. If we hadn't cleared the pot, I'd likely still be at the table helping myself to fourths and fifths!

"How about *Finding Nemo?*" Abigail asked with her remote pointed at the TV undecidedly. "Little Owen loves the fish tank at his pediatrician's office.

Suddenly, I was quite grateful that Gavin hadn't served us fish fry that evening in light of Abigail's film choice. We set Owen up on the floor with far more toys than a child his age could ever need. He crawled back and forth after them, rising to stand on shaky little toes a few times before plopping back down on his diapered bottom. Only occasionally did he look to the little orange fish on the screen, but each time he did, he gave us a huge gummy grin which, to me, counts *Nemo* among our success.

The cartoon film had just introduced us to a gnarly pod of sea turtles when my phone began to ring.

"Oh, not tonight, Dad. It's family night!" Abigail protested.

Seeing as I was feeling mighty comfortable right where I was seated, I let the phone stay in my pocket and the call go to voicemail.

But then it rang again.

Abigail paused the movie and sighed. "Go ahead. It might be important."

Though I hadn't yet received a call from this number, it was one I'd saved all the same—and it belonged to none other than Harmony King.

I pressed to answer the call, but before I could even say hello, a stifled cry met my ears. "Harmony?" I asked, panic gripping my old, worried heart. "Is everything okay?"

She cried more than spoke, but still I managed to understand two very important words. "He's here."

I didn't have to ask who he was. Instantly I knew that it was that same fellow she'd run so far to escape. As far as I was concerned, *Danger* would have been a better name for him than *Alan*.

"Call Nolan," I told Abigail and Gavin. "And the police. Send them to Mrs. Clementine's."

They both sprung to action while I stayed on the line with Harmony.

"Where are you? Where is he?"

Her voice was a little surer now, a little easier to understand. "He's at the front door. I ran upstairs to my room, locked the door, and am hiding under the bed."

Good, so they had at least two locked doors between them. Still, this man had broken in on her before, and I had no doubt that he'd do it again.

"Hurry," I mouthed to Abigail who was on the phone with the police.

"Where's Mrs. Clementine?" Fear tightened around me like a noose. I had to make sure my old friend wasn't also in harm's way. I didn't know Alan well enough to determine whether he'd stoop to hurting her, too, on his path to Harmony.

"Out," Harmony whispered. "I don't know where. Muffin's with me under the bed."

"Good, good. Stay put. The police and Nolan are on their way."

Gavin caught my eye and shook his head. "I couldn't get Nolan, so I left a voicemail."

"The police are on their way," I updated Harmony. Praying, praying, praying for their quick arrival on the scene.

"I'm so—" Harmony's words were cut off by a loud, shrill string of barks.

If Alan hadn't already discovered her, then surely Muffin had just given away that poor girl's location.

The line went dead.

CHAPTER 31

HARMONY

M uffin slipped free of Harmony's grip and began barking like a maniac. The door downstairs creaked open and, soon after, heavy footsteps hurried toward her room.

"Please, God. Please," she prayed through the tears, unsure exactly what she was asking. Perhaps it was that Alan would change his mind, give up, move on—then no one would have to get hurt in this.

Her Chihuahua companion whined and scratched frantically at the door, leading the intruder right to her.

She felt too terrified to call out to him, to look for a weapon with which she could defend herself, to do anything other than cry.

The doorknob rattled but didn't open.

A knock on the door came next.

Harmony covered her mouth with both hands to silence her sobs. If she could just stay hidden for a few more minutes, the police would come to save her.

Her phone buzzed beside her with an incoming call, and the buzzing against the carpet seemed to ring out like thunder.

She hadn't even realized she'd dropped the call with Pastor Adam, but now Nolan was calling her back and possibly sealing her fate.

Oh, God, save me.

"Harmony?" Nolan's voice was among the last she expected to hear on the other side of that door. Could it really be him? Where was Alan? She'd seen him with her own eyes right through the living room window before she'd run to hide in her locked room. Had he really gone?

"Nolan?" she chanced, her voice a nasal moan like as if she were trying to hold back a sneeze.

"Yeah, it's me," he responded with another useless turn of the doorknob. She'd never heard a sweeter sound. Nolan's voice meant she was safe, just as he'd promised. "Are you okay?" he asked with another rap on the door.

Harmony freed herself from under the bed almost as quickly as she'd initially dived beneath it. Stumbling to the door as quick as her shaking legs would take her, she sobbed freely. And then, a moment later, they were together at the threshold to her room.

Muffin let out a deep, throaty bark, and it almost sounded like he was reprimanding Nolan for not making it there fast enough.

Harmony laughed through the tears and pushed her face into Nolan's strong chest. "Pastor Adam said he couldn't reach you. How did you get inside? How did you know to come?" she mumbled into his shirt.

Nolan swayed gently with her and stroked her hair just as he had done upon learning she'd never eaten s'mores. Oh, how that memory now seemed a million miles away. "Mrs. Clementine once showed me where she keeps the spare key in that stone garden frog. I had to get to you, and you weren't answering the door."

"But how did you know I was in trouble?" Did it matter? All that mattered now was that he was here and Alan wasn't. And yet he'd be back again soon. She knew that beyond a shadow of a doubt. Now that she'd come face to face with her ex here in Charleston, she felt the fear even deeper in her bones.

"Megan." Nolan tensed upon speaking his sister's name, and without even looking at his face, Harmony could feel just how angry he'd become. "She called me

up in a panic, saying she may have done something wrong."

Harmony pulled away from him and went to sit on the bed. Her legs felt too weak to hold her for another second. "She told Alan where I live?" she asked in disbelief.

"She didn't mean to." He crossed his arms as tension rolled off him in waves. "But she made a very stupid choice."

Harmony, too, felt her fear turning to anger. "How? What happened?" she demanded.

"Remember how I told you she works at Publix?"

Harmony nodded and hugged a still very distressed and shaking Muffin to her chest. *Calm down, calm down,* she willed herself. If Megan had put her in danger, then at least Nolan had come in an attempt to save her. It had been an honest mistake, though. And Nolan was right—a stupid one.

He shook his head and frowned. "A man came into the store asking around about you. He said he was an old friend and eager to reconnect with you."

"And she believed him?" Harmony spat. *It's not his fault. Control your temper.*

"Afraid so. She told him exactly where to find you. It didn't even occur to her that the man might've been lying until a coworker came to talk to her about the creepy guy trying to find Harmony King. That's when she called me."

"Oh my gosh," Harmony cried. "She can't just tell people where I live! That's gotta be illegal!" The cops were on their way. They'd know whether what Megan did was punishable.

"I'm so sorry, and Megan is, too. Tell me what I can do to make things better."

Harmony ran through the countless options in her mind. It made the most sense to pack her bags and leave, go somewhere Alan wouldn't know to look for her. But she was sick of running every time life got a little hard. Sure, Alan was more than just a small threat, but if she ran away from the good things that she'd begun to build here in Charleston, he'd still be controlling every aspect of her life—just like he wanted.

"He wasn't here when you arrived?" she asked. She needed to focus on the facts, on staying safe going forward, not getting revenge on Megan for her stupidity.

Nolan appeared almost apologetic. "No, I didn't see him."

"He'll be back, and probably soon now that he knows where I live now."

"Then I'll be here, too. This is partially my fault.

If I hadn't made you meet with my sister at the potluck, none of this would be happening now."

Harmony felt disconnected from her emotions as she spoke, but at least she'd managed to tamp the anger down. "No, he would have found me eventually. I have no doubt about that."

Now it was Nolan who seemed afraid. "And what would you have done if he got to you this time? What are you going to do when he finds you next time?"

"I don't know," she admitted.

He sank down onto the bed beside her and ran his hands through his hair. "That's not good enough, Harmony."

"I'm sorry, but it's the truth. I've never been in this situation before."

"With a crazy ex stalking you?"

"Well, yeah, but also not wanting to leave. Earlier I would have just run away to somewhere new, but I don't want to go."

He regarded her for a moment, neither smiling nor frowning. His face gave nothing away. Finally, Nolan said, "I don't want you to go, either."

CHAPTER 32

HARMONY

Harmony and Muffin walked with Nolan downstairs to the living room. The fear she'd felt just minutes earlier clung to her bedroom like an odious perfume, and she didn't want to stay in there any longer than she had to.

True to his word, Nolan refused to leave, even after Harmony assured him she would be okay. A lie, but still she hated how her problems had taken on a life of their own, ensnaring all those around her who had dared to care. Unbelievably, she even felt kind of bad for Megan who had unwittingly put her in such danger. She'd be beside herself with guilt, no doubt.

Yes, normally Harmony would have wasted no time in calling someone up who'd done her wrong to give them a loud and colorful piece of her mind. But what was the point this time around? The only person she really needed to have it out with was Alan, and he'd find her sooner rather than later.

A shiver wracked through her again. She hadn't asked for this, didn't want it, and yet, it was the biggest constant in her life.

The fear, the running, the anger.

How badly she wanted to put all of them behind now that she had begun to rebuild her life. When faced with the very real possibility of losing everything she'd come to care about, she realized just how much she did care—and in a way, that terrified her, too.

Loving people meant giving them power over you. Alan was proof enough of that. Still, even if Virginia, Nolan, Jolene, Abigail, or Pastor Adam never intended to hurt her, they could easily do so by accident just as she could hurt them—just as she had by putting them all in danger now.

It wasn't long until Virginia showed up. She reached the house just as the police were packing up to say goodbye after their short visit.

"We'll keep you informed," the nice officer said with a sympathetic nod.

"Oh, dear!" Virginia cried the very moment the pair of policemen secured the front door behind them. "You must have been terrified. I'm sorry I wasn't here. I mean, I had no idea until Pastor Adam called me."

Harmony felt terrible all over again. Guilt, just like fear, proved to be an emotion in abundant supply. "Ginny," she said. "I'm so sorry I put you in harm's way. I had hoped he wouldn't come looking for me, but I should've known better."

"Hush, say nothing of it. It's not your fault, you poor, poor thing."

Nolan stood and made eyes toward the kitchen. "Mrs. Clementine, may I please have a word with you in private?"

The old woman looked disoriented for a second before nodding and following him out of the room, leaving Harmony alone with her Chihuahua.

"You wouldn't have let anything happen to me. Right, Muffin?" she whispered, stroking the dog's short fur. Her best defenses now would be quick thinking and this five pound warrior pup, Heaven help her.

But she just couldn't continue to put the people she cared about in harm's way. Maybe it would be better if did leave town, after all. This time, though, she wouldn't be running away from a life that had never fit her. She'd be preserving one she'd come to love deeply.

Virginia came back into the living room and sat beside Harmony on the sofa. "Well, then. Shall we work on our knitting projects for a while?"

The front door opened and shut, drawing Harmony's eyes toward the window where she caught a peek of Nolan's head bobbing across the front yard. It was the same window through which she'd spotted Alan earlier that day.

"Don't you worry," Virginia said, patting her on the knee. "He'll be back just as soon as he collects his things." Yes, the same could be said of Alan, too.

Harmony looked at her landlady askance.

Virginia got up to retrieve their yarn and needles, explaining as she went, "I offered him one of the spare bedrooms upstairs, but he says he'd feel much better sleeping on the couch beside Pancake."

So Nolan would be... moving in with them? Mrs. Clementine seemed pleased with this idea, and Harmony didn't want to disappoint her since she'd been the one to lead them all into trouble with her foolish secrecy.

"Thank you for being such a good friend to me," she said solemnly as the older woman handed Harmony her work in progress. She already knew there'd be no point in arguing Nolan's decision. Besides, she really would feel safer having him nearby.

Virginia sat back down, but kept her eyes fixed on her lap as she spoke. "I know you don't think it, because of this whole situation with your ex-boyfriend, but you've been a very good friend to me, too." She paused for a moment before adding, "Almost like the daughter I never had."

Harmony felt tears begin to prick in the corners of her eyes again. Kinder words had never been spoken to her, nor had they ever meant more. All her life she'd longed for a family, and now somehow she'd managed to find one when she wasn't even looking.

It wasn't pretend or imaginary like her relationship had been with Pastor Adam growing up. This sweet and giving woman sitting beside her now truly cared for her.

Her! The girl no one had ever wanted growing up, the damaged soul who had brought danger lurking into their lives.

Virginia Clementine had opened up her home and her heart when Harmony had so little to offer in return. It was she who had set down the roots that bound Harmony to this place, and it was because of her that Harmony couldn't run away scared now.

Not when she finally had something worth fighting for.

In that moment, despite the terrifying visit from Alan and despite the inevitable confrontation brewing, Harmony realized she'd later look back on this as one of the very best days of her life.

CHAPTER 33

HARMONY

The next day Nolan escorted Harmony to work at the diner while Pastor Adam showed up at the house to take care of some church business with Mrs. Clementine. Both dogs, of course, kept a watchful eye over everyone.

Alan didn't come back around that day, which felt like a relief and a disappointment wrapped into one. They both knew he'd be back. What she didn't know was why he'd chosen to wait or where he'd taken up residence while he bided his time.

"Stop thinking about it," Nolan said rather abruptly on their drive home after work. "I can see your thoughts keep going back to him, and you need to cut it out."

Harmony let out a sarcastic laugh. "Easy for you to say. You're not the one he's after, and besides, you're so big, you could probably just step on the guy and squash him like a bug."

Nolan snorted. "If only."

Pastor Adam was still at the house when the two of them returned from their shift at O'Brien's and a bit of "getting her mind off things" around the city. Abigail, Gavin, and little Owen had also joined them, and everyone appeared to be in good spirits.

"Um, guys," Harmony said gently. "This seems like a really bizarre reason to throw a party."

Abigail laughed and shook her head. "You're right about that. We're just here to pick up Dad and then we'll be on our way. Otherwise, he'd never leave just so long as Mrs. Clementine keeps feeding him her delicious cooking."

The pastor put both hands on his belly and puffed out his cheeks. "My daughter knows me so well."

"I'll send some with you to go," Virginia promised from her spot at the stove. It wasn't even four o'clock yet, but apparently she'd started—and nearly finished—prepping dinner all the same.

Meanwhile, Abigail stepped closer to Harmony with a drawn expression on her face. "How are you holding up?"

"I'm fine. It's everyone else I worry about." Harmony attempted a smile, but it refused to come.

"You don't always have to be strong. Sometimes it's okay to let others take care of you, too. Believe me, I learned that the hard way." She gave Harmony a hug that was cut short by commotion near the door.

They both turned to see Abigail's little boy crawling fast toward the doorway, making a beeline for all the interesting shoes piled there.

"I don't think so, little one!" she scolded, luckily saving her son before he could put one of Harmony's work shoes into his waiting mouth.

"Give 'em here," Nolan said, holding his arms out to accept the toddler. "I've got a knack for them when they're this age."

"Enjoy!" Abigail said, plopping her son into Nolan's outstretched arms.

Something very strange happened in Harmony's chest as she watched her friend lift the baby up high into the air and make zooming airplane noises as they dipped from side to side.

Owen giggled nonstop, encouraging all the adults to stop and watch the happy little boy who was completely oblivious to the scary situation that had put the rest of them on edge.

"Dinner's ready!" Virginia announced a short time later. The clock had only just struck four.

"And that's our cue to get out of here," Abigail said, accepting her son back from Nolan. "Thanks for watching him. I can tell you're one of his favorite people now."

"Aww, and he's one of mine," Nolan said, rubbing the wild tuft of bright orange hair on top of the adorable kiddo's head.

"Wait," Pastor Adam urged. "Mrs. Clementine hasn't packed our to-go box yet."

"We're not taking a to-go box," Abigail said, drawing one hand to her hip and staring her old man down.

"Then we can stay?" the pastor asked hopefully.

"Not when we have a nice salad waiting for us at your house," Gavin interjected, sending a knowing look to his future father-in-law.

"But who wants salad when you can have this fine sugared ham instead?"

"Your heart, for one," Abigail said. "Your poor overstretched pants for another."

"Do you hear how she talks to me?" Pastor Adam asked Harmony with a dejected look upon his face.

"She does have a point," Virginia said. "Your waistline has seen better days."

"*Et tu*, Mrs. Clementine?" he asked in mock hurt.

"And it's about time, too," Abigail said triumphantly, nudging her father, fiancé, and son toward the door. "Welcome to Team Healthy Dad, Mrs. Clementine. Goodnight, Harmony and Nolan."

Nolan and Harmony joined Virginia at the table and began to dish up. Yes, it was far too early for dinner, but Ginny had worked hard on this meal and now needed someone to enjoy it with her, seeing as the original intended had been forced away before he could take even a single bite.

Their hostess sat quietly contemplating the ham and au gratin potatoes before her. "Do you think it's my fault that the pastor has become a bit hefty these days? He looks just fine to me, but if his heart is in trouble... I'd hate to be the one to push him toward the grave. He's such a good, kind man. The congregation needs him for as long as they can keep him."

Nolan shook his head vigorously and waved his fork in protest. "What? No way. As a fellow cook, I can tell you that it's our job to make the food as delicious as possible. It's his job to control how much of it he eats."

"Actually, that seems more like it's Abigail's job," Harmony pointed out.

Virginia didn't join in the laughter that followed.

She seemed genuinely distraught and surprised by the fact that Pastor Adam could stand to lose a few —*okay, more than a few*—pounds. "Well, I'd hate for the poor man to be deprived. Maybe I can work out some lighter versions of some of his favorite dishes. Do you think that would help?"

Harmony studied her friend. Clearly, this matter was of the utmost importance to her and needed to be figured out right then and there. "I think he'd love that," she said, wondering if Mrs. Clementine didn't also sometimes imagine roles for Pastor Adam that he didn't actually serve. It was really too bad Virginia was already married, because she and the pastor made quite a happy and well-matched pair.

Virginia nodded and speared a piece of meat with her fork. "Well, then, that's decided. We're all going on a diet… Um, starting tomorrow."

"Nooooooo," Nolan playfully shouted, but then winked at her and took a giant bite of his potatoes. "Seeing as I'm staying here for the indeterminate future, I'd love to help in any way I can," he offered once he'd swallowed down his food.

Harmony sat silent and watched the two of them carry on. It felt just like a real family with everyone helping everyone, all while gently and lovingly teasing each other.

How had she managed to live so long without this?

And now that she knew how this felt...

How could she ever bear to be without it again?

CHAPTER 34

HARMONY

That evening the hours stretched on endlessly before them. Following their early dinner, Mrs. Clementine set to work scouring her recipe cards for substitutions she could make to create modified healthy versions of the meals Pastor Adam liked best.

This left Harmony with Nolan, Muffin, and Pancake, and several hours before any reasonable person would turn in for the night. Harmony also felt as if it were her job to occupy their house guest, since he was, after all, there as a favor to her.

"Want to walk the dogs?" Nolan suggested when neither could find any shows they wanted to watch on TV. She'd have to talk to Virginia about the wonders of Netflix and Hulu someday soon, although she doubted very much the old woman would appreciate a reason to be more sedentary—especially now that she'd jumped feet first into this new health kick.

Harmony glanced at Muffin who popped up and wagged his tail like a tiny rudder. He seemed to get all the exercise he needed without even needing to leave the house, but the larger Irish Wolfhound who currently resided here, too, would definitely need the chance to stretch his legs. As much as Harmony would rather stay put knowing that Alan was somewhere nearby and waiting to strike, it seemed a good idea to get out of the house a bit.

Fresh air being good for you and all that.

Besides, Nolan and the dogs would protect her, if it came right down to it. She knew that now.

"Sure. Let's go," she said, heading to the coat closet to fish out her sneakers.

Once they were outside, each holding onto a leash for one of their comically mismatched dogs, Harmony closed her eyes and sucked in a deep, cool breath of early spring air.

"Pancake likes to run, but I'll try to keep him at a decent pace," Nolan explained, already straining against the behemoth dog who wanted to give chase to a squirrel he'd spied near the edge of the yard.

"Actually, let's go fast," she said, surprising herself.

It would feel nice to run off some of her anxiety, even though she'd never been much a fan of exercise before.

They all picked up the pace, but after a block, it was clear that Muffin's short legs stood no chance of keeping up with the lanky Wolfhound.

"Well, we can speed walk a little at least," she offered with an apologetic shrug. Moving fast also meant that they didn't have to talk quite as much. Even though Harmony felt safe with her friend, she was afraid of the feelings she'd begun to glimpse just beneath the surface of that friendship.

When they'd first met, Nolan had made his interest in her clear, and it seemed his attraction to her was still there. But how did Harmony feel? After making such a horrible mistake in choosing her last boyfriend, she was afraid to trust herself again. Nolan had become such a good friend. Did she really want to risk losing him for the chance that they could build something more?

Knowing herself, she'd probably freak out and ruin things right away, losing both the deep friendship and the possibility of an even deeper love.

"You seem lost in thought," Nolan pointed out, his breathing hardly labored at all despite the brisk exercise.

Lost.

That was a good way to describe it, for she didn't have any answers no matter how hard she tried to find them. She didn't know when Alan would be back or what he'd do once the two of them came face to face. She didn't know whether she could trust herself to love Nolan, no matter how good he'd been to her. And she didn't know how she could carry forward in both situations without horribly messing something up, something important. Like the lives of people she cared about.

"What are you thinking about?" Nolan asked with a tilt of his jaw.

"Alan," she answered simply. It was partially true and seemed like the easiest way out of a conversation she wasn't quite ready to have yet. Or ever.

"But you're smiling." He nudged her slightly, forcing her to look up at him.

"I am?"

Nolan nodded. "Here and there, mixed in with your usual frowns."

"Hmm," she responded simply.

"Now you have to tell me," he insisted with a piercing gaze that made her cheeks burn hot.

"I have to?" she asked sarcastically. If only he knew, he'd likely change his mind. If ever the time existed for the two of them to have the relationship talk, this was not it. Too many other things were currently unresolved. They needed to focus on dealing with Alan first, and then Harmony could decide whether she felt courageous enough to admit her new feelings.

"Yes, enlighten me. Tell me about those thoughts that are running through your busy, busy mind." He smiled, but she couldn't return the gesture. Why did everything have to be so confusing? Why was the only thing she could count on right now the fact that Alan would find her?

Should she tell Nolan how much his protection meant to her? That it made her realize things she wasn't ready to admit aloud?

Maybe she could get by with a partial truth. "I'm just thinking that other than this Alan situation—which, yes, is a hugely negative thing—I'm actually really happy."

He scrunched up his face and regarded her like she'd lost her mind. Maybe she had. "That's kind of weird," Nolan said with a quizzical glance.

"It is, isn't it?" She shrugged. "I don't know. I guess I just like my life these days. And the people in it."

"Well, we like you right back," he said, erasing the

doubt from his face and flashing her an enormous grin. "Is that all you were thinking about?"

"What do you mean is that all?" Harmony hissed at him. "It's plenty!"

He shrugged. "Just seems like you're holding something back."

"How do you know me so well already?" She couldn't help but laugh despite her worry.

"It's a gift." He picked up the pace, forcing Harmony to do the same.

Once she'd caught up, she shot him a scalding glance. "Really. I'm serious. I want to know. Tell me how you do that."

"I just pay attention. I see you and your strawberry, marshmallow, gingersnap goodness, and you just make sense to me in a way little else has before."

Harmony giggled, then gasped for breath. "We should really make s'mores again sometime soon. I'm afraid you've got me hooked."

"See, I knew there was a reasonable person in there somewhere."

Good, he'd picked up on the change of topic. This man really did love him some s'mores, and it seemed he had started to love Harmony, too. Even though he no longer pressured her for dates and she needed more time to sort out her past before she could focus on even the chance of a future...

She realized then that, when the timing was finally right, she wanted to be with Nolan now and forever.

CHAPTER 35

PASTOR ADAM

Abigail and Gavin were dead serious about that salad, and regrettably had a second to go with it the next day. Even given all of eternity, I'll never quite understand the appeal of vegetables served without salt and butter. Now that Mrs. Clementine had turned on me, too, it looked like I'd really, truly be losing some weight and in the very near future.

Lord, give me strength. I can do all things through You. Yes, even this... Right?

As I was pouring myself a cup of coffee and adding organic soy milk to the mix—yes, organic soy milk, a double sin against my poor, sweet morning cuppa—my phone buzzed with a call from Mrs. Clementine.

"I'm not happy with you," I said, admittedly pouting.

"Oh, stop," she cajoled. "You act like losing weight is the worst thing that's ever happened to you."

She and I knew that, as unbearable as this diet was already proving to be, I'd suffered much worse during my days on this earth. The first awful thing was losing Abigail's mother—not to the Maker, but to her own wanderlust. We're still married to this day, though I haven't seen her in more than twenty years. The second horrible thing occurred when we lost Abigail's husband, Owen, during his service to our country.

Considering these events, I supposed I could get through a bit of bland eating. Didn't mean I needed to be happy about it, though.

"If it makes you feel any better," she continued, "I'm already adapting some new, healthy versions of all your favorites. Nolan has offered to help, too."

As a matter of fact, this news did make me feel better. For even if I had a worryingly low amount of butter and salt in my diet for the next few weeks, at least I had love and support by the heaping spoonful.

"That Nolan is a nice boy," I told Mrs. Clementine while rummaging in the cabinets for some powdered creamer or other hidden beverage fixings.

"So nice," my friend agreed. "And so good for our Harmony."

I bobbed my head. "Those two already love each other like crazy. Have you noticed?"

Mrs. Clementine sounded offended by the question. "Of course I have," she scolded. "Everyone in the tri-county area has probably noticed by now."

"You mean except for Harmony herself," I corrected with a chuckle.

She sighed. "Funny, isn't it? She has the perfect partner right in front of her nose and she can't be bothered to see it."

"I'd say she's probably keeping her eyes closed on purpose. Sometimes good things can be just as scary as the bad."

"Mmm," she responded, and we both reflected on this thought for a moment. I jotted down a reminder for myself to explore this as a possible topic for a future sermon.

"How's Muffin?" I asked, not ready to say goodbye just yet because it would leave me alone with subpar coffee and my worried diet obsession.

"Such a sweet little house guest," Mrs. Clementine cooed. "But he is just a guest. Isn't he? When do you suppose his work with Harmony will be done?"

I thought about this for a second to make sure I was content with my answer. "It'll be done when it's done."

"How very philosophical of you." I could just picture my friend rolling her eyes at me from halfway across the city. "And how will we know when that time comes?"

"The Lord will tell us when it's time, and I reckon Muffin will as well."

CHAPTER 36

HARMONY

Harmony chatted with Jolene as they prepared to open O'Brien's for breakfast that morning. She found the familiarity of their routine comforting as she filled the condiment caddies and Jolene put the coffee on. Today was Saturday, their busiest day of the week, and Harmony looked forward to losing herself in the hustle and bustle of the busy restaurant.

"Carolina called me up last night and said she's been offered a paid internship at her college. Can you believe it? My baby, an intern!" Jolene spoke of her daughter so often that Harmony felt as if they were already dear friends despite not having had the chance to meet her just yet.

"Congrats. That's wonderful. Carolina must be as

smart as they come." She went to write out the day's specials on the chalkboard by the door while Jolene continued to work with the coffee.

"She sure is. No idea where she gets it from, but she is certainly making the most of it since heading off to school." Jolene paused and chewed on her lower lip. It was clear how much she missed her little girl despite wanting to be supportive of her big city dreams.

"Well, she's lucky to have a mom like you," Harmony offered with a reassuring smile. She'd had dreams like that once, that a simple change of location could give her a whole new life. Good on Carolina for actually making it happen.

"Oh, look at the time!" the other waitress cried. "I got so busy boasting that we forgot to open up the restaurant on time."

Harmony glanced up at the clock above the kitchen and—sure enough—they'd missed opening time by five whole minutes. When she went to answer the door, she found a few expectant diners waiting to be given reprieve from the chilly morning air.

"Good morning," she told them each as they shrugged out of their jackets and hung them on the old-fashioned coat rack by the door. "Take a seat where ever you'd like, and we'll come 'round with the coffee in a moment."

Jolene was already on it, wielding a pot in each hand. They'd already set out mugs and creamers on each table, which made getting started with their first batch of customers quick and efficient. It was part of the reason folks liked O'Brien's so much. They never had to wait to get fresh coffee and great eats.

Nolan's face popped into view through the kitchen window. "Can I get something started?"

"Hold your horses!" Jolene called from across the way, and Harmony chuckled at their easy banter. That's how life felt here, she realized, *easy*. Well, except for all the unwanted drama she'd brought with her from Alabama.

The front door swung open again and another group of diners entered.

"Good morning and welcome!" Harmony and Jolene both called in unison.

The group smiled and nodded, then took a booth near the large window that overlooked the street. A lone customer also entered behind them, keeping his head tucked down as he proceeded to the far corner of the dining room. Even without getting a clear view of his face, Harmony knew exactly who'd just arrived at O'Brien's—and that he wasn't here for breakfast.

This ends now, she told herself, striding forward with far more confidence than she felt. Hopefully no one else would be able to see the way her breaths came out as short, desperate puffs or that her chest had tightened so severely it felt as if her heart would burst.

"I heard you were looking for me," she told Alan with a biting stare as she slapped down a menu in front of him. "What do you want?"

He kept his eyes glued to the table and muttered, "The same thing I've always wanted—*us.*"

This man right here was the one she'd once loved, although that now felt like a lifetime ago. How could she have been so blind? Was she really so desperate for someone to belong to that she was willing to settle for someone who had never been right for her—and who clearly also wasn't quite right in the head, either?

"You and I? We're no longer an us," she told him in a low growl, feeling the fear ebb out of her the longer and more insistently she confronted him. Emboldened enough to go forward, she preferred not to draw the attention of the other diners or to worry Jolene and Nolan if she could handle the situation herself.

"I'm sorry I hurt you," he said, finally looking up at her with the pleading blue eyes she had once found so alluring. Now they seemed icy and threatening rather than beautiful. "That wasn't supposed to happen."

She crossed her arms to form a shield over her heart and show him she wouldn't be backing down. Not this time. "Yeah, well, it did happen, and it's not just something I can forget about."

"But you *can* forgive me. Please, it's all I ever wanted—for us to be together." Despite the emotion in his words, Alan didn't cry, didn't even frown. He merely voiced his thoughts plainly all while keeping a watch for her reaction. In a way, this version of Alan was even more intimidating than the loud, violent beast she knew he could become when pushed hard enough. But this wasn't about what he claimed to want, it was about Harmony and what she needed—and that was to be free of him once and for all.

"No, Alan," she said, casting a pity frown his way. "My life is here now."

"This isn't a life, Harmony," he hissed as he spread his palms out flat on the table before him then took a deep, measured breath. "It's just a vacation. Your real life is back with me in Mobile. We can still be happy. Give us another chance."

His rage began to bubble beneath the surface, and

soon it would be boiling over. They were in a public place, though. He couldn't hurt her here.

She pressed forward with her arguments, willing him to understand and give up of his own volition before things escalated further. "I'm not entirely sure we were ever happy to begin with. I've made up my mind and I'd thank you to stop pestering me. I'm not going back, and I don't want to be with you."

He shook his head and looked down at his hands, still splayed on top of the table as if he were bracing himself for something. "You're so different now. This isn't my Harmony."

"Correct, I'm not your anything. I'm my own person and I get to make my own choices. I'm choosing not to be with you. I don't want to be your wife, your girlfriend, your anything. In fact, I never want to see you again."

And suddenly, he became kind and placating again. "C'mon, don't be like that. I've given you time to come to your senses, and now it's time to come home." He reached up and tried to take her hand, but she yanked it away before he could make contact.

"I'm not going anywhere with you," she said, loud enough that some of the other customers had started to sneak glances their way. She caught Jolene's eye, and she nodded and walked calmly to the back of the house.

"I've come all this way to get you back. Not just today, but I've been trying on every day I've had off from work. Do you know how much driving that is just to be turned down?" His hands began to shake. His skin became ruddy.

"I'm sorry you wasted your time, but we're over. You made sure of that the last time I saw you." She shuddered at the memory of his crazed declaration that she was already his wife, that they should…

Never again. She'd ignored too many warning signs, been such a fool.

"I said I was sorry," Alan told her, his brows knitting together in frustration. And then he began to rise to his feet.

"And she said you need to leave. Now I'm saying it, too. Get yourself out of here, or I'll do it for you." Nolan appeared at her side, a towering presence that comforted her but should have terrified Alan.

If Alan was afraid, though, he didn't show it. Instead, he pulled himself the rest of the way to his feet and stared Nolan down. "You think I don't know who you are? You think you can just swoop in and steal my girl right out from under me?"

That was when the first punch connected straight

with Nolan's nose. A terrifying thwack reverberated throughout the restaurant.

Jolene grabbed Harmony by the waist and pushed with all her might until they were both safely hidden in the kitchen…

Leaving Nolan to take care of Alan on his own.

CHAPTER 37

HARMONY

Harmony struggled against Jolene's determined grip. The larger woman clutched her tightly from behind, refusing to let Harmony leave the kitchen.

"But it's *my* fight," she argued. "I have to make sure Nolan's okay!"

Jolene talked calmly despite Harmony's struggle. "Fighting ain't always the right thing. Let Nolan handle it until the cops show up."

"The police?" Did that mean it would all be over within minutes? Could they make Alan leave her alone for good? Harmony went lax in her friend's arms.

"Yes, I called them and they're already on their

way. It's almost over, baby." Jolene's hold relaxed enough for Harmony to break free.

"I'm sorry. I have to be there!" she called back, knowing the other waitress had only been doing what she could to keep her safe. But it wouldn't be fair for Nolan to bear the brunt of Alan's anger. He'd never done a single thing wrong and didn't deserve this.

Passing back into the dining room, her eyes zoomed straight to the back corner where one of the customers now held Alan back so he couldn't hit Nolan again. From the looks of the smug smirk on Alan's face, he was the only one who had managed to throw any punches in the brief time Harmony had been kept away.

"Stop!" she shouted, forcing herself between them.

It was clear the customer wouldn't be able to keep Alan back much longer. Determination gleamed in his cold eyes.

"Stay back." Nolan pushed her behind him so that he was the one facing Alan's fury head on.

"This is the guy you want over me?" her ex challenged.

"It's not like that," she whimpered, terrified of what he might do next.

"Oh, please," he growled. "I followed you enough

to figure things out. You spend every waking hour with this guy. Looks like he's been sleeping over, too. Funny, cuz that whole time we were together you claimed to be saving yourself. But now you seem just fine jumping into bed with the first loser who came along."

"Alan," she sobbed. "Please stop. Please go away."

"I believe the lady made herself clear," Nolan said through gritted teeth, though he kept both hands extended downward in a gesture of peace. "If you leave now, you won't have to explain yourself to the police."

Nobody said anything for a moment.

"Okay?" Nolan urged.

Alan still didn't respond, but stopped struggling to break free.

Nolan nodded, and the customer released Alan from his hold.

He immediately took another swing at Nolan, connecting with his jaw and forcing him to hunch over in pain.

The customer tried to grab Alan again, but he fought him off and continued to advance toward Nolan, punching, kicking, spitting, doing whatever he could to hurt the other man.

Nolan pulled himself back up to his full height

but didn't return his opponent's advances. He just took one hit after the next while Harmony screamed and cried.

Jolene advanced from the safety of the kitchen and helped the customer regain hold of Alan. They each managed to hold him by an arm while the other diners watched wordlessly as this horror unfolded before them.

Harmony continued to try to appeal to Alan's better judgment. He had once been kind, once been someone she loved. It didn't have to be like this, but he was the only one who could stop it. "Alan, you can't force me to be with you, and even if you could, this is not the way to do it. Please, please just go away and stay away."

He laughed and attempted to jerk his arm away from Jolene, but she held on tight, her freshly manicured nails digging into his bare arm so hard they left little pinpoints in his skin. "How can I leave with your friends keeping me in this sucker hold?"

She looked to Nolan who collapsed onto the nearest bench seat, clutching at his jaw which had already bloomed with ugly purples and blues. A trickle of blood dripped from his nose and ran down his chin.

Meanwhile, Alan appeared completely unscathed, save for the indents from Jolene's fingernails.

"Are you okay?" Harmony asked, taking a step closer to her boss, her friend, her Nolan, and feeling so terrible that he'd taken such a beating at her expense.

Why hadn't he fought back? He had every right given the scene Alan had caused in the restaurant, given that Alan had thrown the first punch, given that Alan was clearly out of his mind.

"Why didn't you defend yourself?" she demanded, almost as angry with Nolan now as she was with Alan. It was so hard seeing his handsome face marred by the gruesome evidence of the other wild man's anger.

"I didn't want you to think I'm like him," Nolan mumbled. Though his voice came out weak and breathless, she understood every single word. He wanted her to know that he would never hurt her, that his love was just that—*love*, pure and simple.

Alan swore up a blue streak, but she no longer cared. The police would be here soon enough to take care of him. It was up to her now to take care of Nolan. That's what people did when they cared for each other. Nolan had taken the full force of the other man's range so that Harmony wouldn't have to.

Despite all her fears, doubts, and reservations, she saw it now. God's true presence lived in Nolan Murphy. When faced with an evil before him, he'd actually turned the other cheek!

The door swung open again, and this time two uniformed police officers charged into the restaurant. She didn't know how much Jolene had told them during their brief phone call, but it wasn't difficult to figure out what had happened here. They marched straight up to Alan and read him his rights.

It was over.

Finally over.

CHAPTER 38

HARMONY

Harmony sat in the booth beside Nolan as the officer took statements from the customers. The other cop had already left with Alan in the backseat of their squad car.

Jolene flipped the sign to read *closed* and brought everyone sequestered inside the restaurant another round of coffee.

"Does it hurt real bad?" Harmony asked Nolan, wincing as she watched him wipe away the last drops of blood from his nose.

He sucked in air through his teeth and tried to smile, but his face was too swollen to complete the gesture. "Nah, I've been in way worse scrapes than this."

Somehow Harmony doubted that, but she didn't

argue the point. This wonderful man had taken quite the beating on her behalf and now minimized his pain to help assuage her guilt.

The female police officer came to speak with them then, and Harmony scooted over to give her space to sit in the booth beside her.

"What a start to the morning," she said with a fleeting grin, then cleared her throat and narrowed her eyes at Harmony. "Can you identify the man who caused the altercation here today?"

"Yes, he's my ex-boyfriend, Alan White. He lives in Mobile, Alabama, but he came here today looking for me."

They exchanged particulars about her history with Alan, what they'd been to each other, what had caused her to run away.

"Were you aware that this same Alan White was arrested in multiple states for prior incidents of domestic abuse and one previous case of assault?"

A sinking feeling swirled in Harmony's gut, but she forced herself to keep her voice steady. "I had no idea, but it makes sense."

So she hadn't been the only one. How many other poor women had been scared and manipulated by Alan? Who were they, and how were they faring now?

Had they managed to escape or…? No, she refused to think the worst.

The officer nodded. "Seems his record goes back clear to his eighteenth birthday. They're sealed before that, but it's possible he had some juvenile infarctions as well."

Harmony head spun as she tried to make sense of it all. Yes, Alan had been cruel to her when they were younger, but he'd been so charming and kind when they'd found each other again as adults. He hadn't grown kinder—just became better at hiding the darkness.

"How did he get by so long with hurting so many people?" she asked, needing to know, needing to understand how this could have gone on for so long.

The officer shook her head slightly, but kept her voice professional. "It seemed he'd stay focused on one victim for a couple years before moving on to the next. He'd get brought in, but no one ever pressed formal charges. A lot of folks are afraid to go through with it, but after he paid a visit to your house, we did some digging and saw a clear pattern of behavior there. Tell me this, how long were the two of you together?"

"About a year." Would Alan really have continued to stalk and plead with her for another year or more before giving up? She hated that her freedom would have meant another woman was cast into the same nightmare she'd just narrowly escaped that day.

Harmony looked to Nolan for encouragement, then said, "And I'd like to press charges."

"I figured you might. I still have more to get through here, but one of us will call you down to the station later today so we can talk in more detail." She nodded at Harmony, then switched her focus to Nolan.

"I'd like to press charges, too. Whatever helps keep him far away from Harmony as long as possible." He didn't have much to add after making this declaration since he only knew about his side of the fight and whatever little Harmony had told him before that day.

It wasn't long before the officer thanked him and headed over to the next table.

"I'm glad you're not backing down," Nolan said, reaching for her hands across the table. "That guy deserves to rot in jail."

She sighed and leaned back in the booth, still clinging to Nolan's hands which, unlike his face, were perfectly untouched. That's what happened when a fight ended up so one-sided. "I'm no expert on the law, but something tells me that even with us pressing charges, there will be no rotting away for Alan. Either he'll move on or he'll be back."

Nolan grimaced at this news, but didn't seem to have any information to add to Harmony's understanding of what was ahead. "Just to be safe, you should get a restraining order."

"Oh, I will," she promised. "But I'm not letting him run me out of my home. I belong here with all of you. It's where I've always belonged."

He squeezed her hands, and she felt the rapid beat of his pulse against her skin. "I'm glad you're staying. Charleston just wouldn't be the same without you."

She forced a laugh. "Oh, please, I'm just one out of more than a hundred thousand people in this city."

Nolan's eyes seemed to dance as he held her in his gaze. "No *just* about it. You're not just one. You're *the one.*"

Her heart leaped in her chest. Earlier she'd been so afraid to have this conversation with him, but now she was glad it had arrived. Watching Nolan defend her from Alan's advances without so much as raising a fist when he could have so easily overpowered the slighter man had cleared any last vestiges of doubt from her mind.

Nolan had never been *just* a friend.

"What are you saying?" she asked him, still afraid but also willing to face that fear. For him.

He lifted the napkin from his face that had been used to staunch the flow of blood and patted to make sure the wound had really finished bleeding out. When his tissue came away clean, he attempted a smile again.

"Isn't it obvious?" he asked. "Ever since that first day in the restaurant when you chewed me out for talking too much… That's how long I've loved you. When that creep was pummeling me with his fists but I knew you were safe, it was okay because I loved you. Right now, I love you. And I want to keep loving you forever, as long as you'll let me. *If* you'll let me."

"There's no ifs here. I love you right on back, Nolan," she told him shyly.

Nolan smiled so big at this news that the contraction of his facial muscles caused him a fresh flash of pain. "Worth it," he said, smiling again just to prove his point.

She chuckled and shook her head. After all this time, after so much worrying, sharing the nature of her feelings with Nolan had been as easy as taking down a breakfast order. It was comforting, familiar, delicious, and exactly what she needed to start the rest of her day—her life—off right.

"You know," she said thoughtfully as Nolan watched her with a smaller, albeit just as goofy grin. "I'd kiss you now if I wasn't worried about causing you more pain."

He leaned in closer to her on the bench seat and whispered, "But it will hurt even more if you don't kiss me. *Right here,* and as we both know, that's the very worst place to hurt."

He took her hand and placed it gently over his chest. His heart beat wildly, and it was all for her. It had always been for her.

Without thinking twice, she leaned forward and pressed a very light kiss against his swollen lips. It wasn't the kind of kiss you got in fairytales, but it was real and perfect and just for them.

CHAPTER 39

HARMONY

Three weeks later

Harmony could hardly believe how quickly her life changed after that fateful day in O'Brien's. Since then, Alan had been arraigned on charges of criminal stalking, domestic abuse, and aggravated assault. The kindly officer from the restaurant had informed her that he'd been unable to make bail and was awaiting his trial date behind bars.

With the immediate threat gone, Nolan and Pancake moved back home, leaving Virginia and Harmony to spend more time developing their close friendship as well. It had been Ginny's idea to start a ladies craft circle through the church, and Harmony had eagerly agreed to co-lead the group even though she was still very much a newbie herself.

She and Nolan saw each other every day at work and a few nights each week for dates or joint ventures to the dog park. Tonight's visit was bittersweet, because it would be their last time bringing Muffin. With his work done, it was time for the special little Chihuahua to return home to his brothers, sister, and mother.

Although Harmony would miss her Muffin dearly, she'd already submitted an application to the local rescue expressing her interest in a wiry little terrier mix that had lived more of its life at the shelter than in anybody's home. She instantly connected with the trembling gray mess of fur that reminded her of a mini Pancake.

But before she could move forward with her adoption of the dog she planned to name "S'moresy," she needed to give sweet little Muffin the perfect send-off. She and Virginia had worked overtime to knit his siblings matching sweaters and hats so that they could also stay warm and stylish, no matter what the weather. Somehow the tiny dog had doubled his belongings in the short time with Harmony, and she wanted to make sure he had every last bit of it when he returned to Pastor Adam's house that evening.

That's why she and Nolan had needed to drive separately tonight. Both trunks were needed!

"Are you going to be okay?" Nolan asked, pressing a kiss to her temple as the two of them watched Pancake and Muffin chase each other through the park.

She nodded and put on as brave a face as she could muster. "It's not like it's goodbye. I've volunteered to help Abigail with the dogs when I can. Kind of my way of paying it forward."

It wouldn't be the same, they both knew that, but Harmony had always known the arrangement with her church dog would be temporary. And to think she hadn't even wanted him in the beginning.

"Muffin, c'mere, baby!" she called, which brought the little dog racing over. She hoisted him into her arms and showered him with kisses on his tiny apple-shaped head. "It's amazing how much love fits into this tiny, little package."

"Just imagine how much fits inside a giant one like Pancake," Nolan teased, scratching his Irish Wolfhound behind the ears.

Harmony set Muffin back down so he could go play, and her boyfriend pulled her into his chest.

"It's a good thing you're doing. You know that, right? Muffin loves you, but he has a great home to return to. That little shelter dog you've had your eye on, though, he needs you. He's never had anyone before, and now that lucky little guy will get to go home with the very best person I know."

"Thanks," she sniffed, refusing to cry. Muffin needed her to be strong.

"It doesn't just have to be that one dog," Nolan continued on. "Maybe one day when we're old and married... You know, like a few months from now, we can rescue one dog for each month I've known and loved you."

"So six?" she asked with a laugh. "Seriously, Nolan. Sometimes you're just ridiculous."

"There's that smile," he said, pulling her into a dancer's pose so they could look into each other's eyes. "I love that smile, but you know, you kind of missed the important part of that last bit I said."

"You mean about the six dogs?"

"That, and..." he nudged.

Harmony twisted up her face as if thinking hard, then sighed. "I have absolutely no idea/ I guess you're going to have to spell it out for me."

"Oh, you are incorrigible," he teased, swaying back and forth with her, neither caring that they were in the middle of a very public place and waiting for Abigail and Pastor Adam to join them.

"What I was saying is that I want to marry you, Miss Harmony King, and soon."

"Are you sure?" she asked. "I mean, I can be a lot to handle. Do you really think you're cut out for the job?"

"So sassy with me now! Can't a man declare his intentions without getting the third degree?"

"Are you sure you really want to marry me?" she asked again. As much as she loved Nolan and knew he loved her, she'd spent her whole life as the girl no one had wanted, the girl without a family. It was still hard to believe this sudden, tremendous change in fortune.

"People don't usually ask so soon, you know," she pointed out, mentally kicking herself for killing this otherwise romantic moment.

He laughed and took a deep breath. "Who says I'm asking? I'm simply letting you know that I plan to ask someday soon. I know how you need a bit of time to get used to some ideas."

She stood on tiptoe to kiss him. "Thanks for letting me know. I will definitely think about saying yes when the time comes."

But Harmony already knew what her answer would be. There was nothing left to think about.

Nolan was the only man she'd ever wanted and the family she'd been waiting her entire life to find.

She'd once believed that people couldn't change, but she now knew better. With a little love, anything was possible.

CHAPTER 40

PASTOR ADAM

Abigail and I both went to the dog park to welcome Muffin back to our fold. When we arrived, we found Harmony and Nolan slow dancing right there in the middle of the park as if no one was watching. It warmed my heart to witness just how far that young woman had come since first returning to our city earlier that year.

"She looks so sad," Abigail said walking beside me. "But so happy, too."

I couldn't help but agree. "That, my dear, is the complex nature of life. Loving means losing, but not loving also means not living."

"That's a good one," my daughter told me, nudging my arm. "You should write that one down to use in a sermon sometime."

I drew out my phone and told that sweet Siri woman what I needed to remember so she could take a note. I still preferred Mrs. Clementine as my secretary, but Abigail had been working hard to get me to use the technology in my life somewhat more effectively.

"Over here!" Harmony called, waving us on over.

"I can't believe today is our last day," she told Abigail, wiping at an invisible tear in the corner of her eye. "You promise I'll be the first you call whenever you need help?"

"Promise," Abigail assured her.

Muffin came running over with his Irish Wolfhound friend. He'd grown a little chunkier since he'd last lived with Abigail and me but, boy, did that dog have hearts in his eyes whenever he looked at Harmony.

Harmony scooped the dog up and buried her face in his short fur.

"It was good for him, too," I told her. "You gave Muffin a purpose and the chance to be his own dog outside of the pack. I can see he loves you dearly."

Harmony sniffed and wiped at another tear. This one was big and fat and raced quickly across the slope of her cheek.

"And I love him dearly. It's funny…" She laughed

here as if to prove her point. "At first I thought you two were crazy, throwing a dog at me the moment I hit town, but now I can see why you did. Loving this little guy opened my heart in a way I hadn't been able to open it before."

"And now you're surrounded by all kinds of love," I said, slapping Nolan on the shoulder. He and I both knew that it wouldn't be long until he managed a proposal. Those two had loved each other first as friends, which made their bond that much stronger. They'd soon be ready to join their lives together under the Lord's watchful protection.

She nodded. "I really am, and I have you to thank for setting it all into motion."

I smiled a big ol' grin. "Not me. The Lord working through me and Abigail and these wonderful, little dogs. And you, too."

"It's funny—once I turned eighteen I thought I'd never step foot in Charleston again, but even after all these years away, it's never stopped being my home. It's like my heart always knew where it belonged even when I didn't."

"God brought you back," I told her. "He never gave up on you. He never gives up on any of us."

"And neither does my dad," Abigail added, offering me a quick peck on the cheek.

Harmony hugged us both, then reluctantly placed Muffin into my waiting arms. "I'm going to miss you, little guy," she cooed. "But I know you're ready to help somebody else now."

And I knew it, too...

I couldn't wait to see how the Lord would work His wonders through our beloved church dogs next.

WHAT'S NEXT?

Carolina Brown couldn't be more different than her mama if she tried—and truthfully, most of us believe she worked hard at precisely that. She worked hard at everything else, too, and set off to college to accomplish big things in the wide world. Unfortunately, God called her right back to Charleston when her mama suffered a near fatal accident that left her requiring round the clock care.

Now that poor young woman reckons her ambitions have reached a dead end. I say it's just a sudden turn toward a new destination she can't quite see yet. If Carolina is ever going to believe in herself enough to reach for happiness a second time, she's going to need some outside encouragement.

It's been a long time since she's come round to the

church, but that's not going to stop me from coming round to her. Sometimes you've gotta meet people part-way, and sometimes you've gotta entrust them with one miracle so they can find the next for themselves.

I do believe Cupcake is the perfect church dog for the job. Now, I'm sure you're wondering, can one little Chihuahua fix two broken lives? Stick around and see for yourself.

Get your copy at www.MelStorm.com/ChurchDogs

AFTERWORD

Home is such a tricky concept. Some people never feel as if they belong in their surroundings while others feel as if they can never leave that special place they've made all their own.

Oh, I definitely had my Harmony period growing up. I hated the small Michigan town I grew up in and could not wait to leave it behind for bigger and better things. Only each time I ventured out toward the big city, I found myself running back for the state that had always fit me perfectly, just like a… mitten.

Like Harmony, the real person I was running from was myself. Sometimes it's easier to look outside and say, "This is the reason I'm not happy. This is the reason I can't find peace."

It's only when we learn to look within, to our hearts, to God, that we can truly find where we're meant to be.

And despite my adolescent wanderings, I'm proud to say that I've settled with my Alaskan husband in my home state of Michigan and just can't picture myself anywhere else in the world.

Sometimes we run so fast, we don't realize we're moving in a circle... but that's exactly what happened to me, and thankfully I love where I've ended up. I love that I'm raising my daughter close enough to my old haunts to take her for a visit. I love that my roots run deep and my home state has become a part of who I am.

Don't get me wrong, I also love visiting Charleston, Anchorage, and Sweet Grove in the books I write, and I visit so many more in those I read as well. But to me, Michigan will always be home, will always have my heart.

How has your hometown defined the person you've become?

Whether you are a product of your upbringing or turned out the exact opposite of how you were raised, take a moment to be grateful for its role in helping you turn into the person you were meant to be.

They call it home sweet home for a reason.

And even when it's more bitter than sweet, there truly is no place like home.

ACKNOWLEDGMENTS

This time around the bend, thanks goes out to all the usual suspects and a few new members of my support system as well. My biggest helpers when it comes to bringing the church dogs to life are first and foremost my two Chihuahua babies, Sky Princess and Mama Mila.

They are the ones who made me fall in love with this tiny dog breed and serve as the basis for the personality and actions of all the doggie goodness this series has to offer. They also stay glued to my side while I write each day, laying cozily in cat baskets on top of my desk or even inside my shirt (which happens to be Sky's favorite place to snuggle). If you've never had a Chihuahua lick the inside of your ear, you are missing one of the most special blessings this life has to offer!

My husband serves as the inspiration for many of my characters and for all of the romance. Yes, even though I'm the romance author, he's the one with the big, loving heart! He's been through some very tough times in his life, but he's emerged on the other side as a strong, faithful man and one heck of a daddy to our little girl. He is also one of the earliest readers of my books, dutifully giving me his feedback even though my stories have a way of making him feel sadness deep-down. I promise to give him a big thank you hug on your behalf, if you find that his sacrifice has been worthwhile.

My other early reader and my Southern inspiration is Angi Hegner, the world's best assistant and friend! Aren't I blessed to have so many world's bests in my life? She reads my chapters as I write them, devours those messy first drafts without so much as batting an eye at the horrible, glaring typos. She gets excited and holds me accountable, too. Without Angi, the books definitely would not get written in a timely manner. That's for sure.

My editor, Megan, is another God-send. She polishes my words and somehow makes my crazy schedule work for the both of us. Mallory Rock brings my stories to life with her art, and the church dog covers are my favorites yet! My proofreaders, Jasmine Jordan and Alice Shepard, are also fantastic at what they do and such a joy to work with.

My brother, Ron, has recently moved in with our family and has helped tremendously by cooking our meals and keeping the house clean, so I can write, write, write. I love you, little bwuzzuh!

And to you, my reader, thank you for enabling me to keep doing what I love each and every day. Thank you for opening your heart to my characters and their stories, and thank you for being wonderful you!

GET TEXT UPDATES

Well, here's something cool… You can now sign up to get text notifications for all my most important book news. You can choose to receive them for New Releases, New Pre-Orders, or Special Sales--or any combination of the three.

These updates will be short, sweet, and to the point with a link to the new book or deal on your favorite retailer.

You choose when you receive them, making this new way of communicating fully customized to your needs as a reader.

Sign up at www.MelStorm.com/TextMe

MORE FROM MELISSA STORM

Sign up for free stories, fun updates, and uplifting messages from Melissa at www.MelStorm.com/gift

* * *

The Church Dogs of Charleston

A very special litter of Chihuahua puppies born on Christmas day is adopted by the local church and immediately set to work as tiny therapy dogs.

Little Loves

Mini Miracles

Dainty Darlings

Tiny Treasures

Bitty Blessings

* * *

The Sled Dog Series

Get ready to fall in love with a special pack of working and retired sled dogs, each of whom change their new owners' lives for the better.

Let There Be Love

Let There Be Light

Let There Be Life

Season of Mercy

Season of Majesty

Season of Mirth

* * *

The First Street Church Romances

Sweet and wholesome small town love stories with the community church at their center make for the perfect feel-good reads!

Love's Prayer

Love's Promise

Love's Prophet

Love's Vow

Love's Trial

Love's Treasure

Love's Testament

Love's Gift

* * *

The Alaska Sunrise Romances

These quick, light-hearted romances will put a smile on your face and a song in your heart. It's time to indulge in a sweet Alaskan get-away!

Must Love Music

Must Love Military

Must Love Mistletoe

Must Love Mutts

Must Love Mommy

Must Love Moo

Must Love Mustangs

Must Love Miracles

Must Love Movie Star

Must Love Mermaids

* * *

The Memory Ranch Romances

This new Sled Dogs-spinoff series harnesses the restorative power of both horses and love at Elizabeth Jane's therapeutic memory ranch.

Memories of Home

Memories of Heaven

Memories of Healing

* * *

The Finding Mr. Happily Ever After Series

One bride, four possible grooms, unlimited potential for disaster to strike. Is the man waiting at the end of the aisle the one that's meant to be Jazz's forever love?

Nathan

Chase

Xavier

Edwin

The Finale

* * *

Sweet Promise Press

What's our Sweet Promise? It's to deliver the heartwarming, entertaining, clean, and wholesome reads you love with every single book.

Saving Sarah

Catching Carol

Flirting with the Fashionista

* * *

Stand-Alone Novels and Novellas

Whether climbing ladders in the corporate world or taking care of things at home, every woman has a story to tell.

A Mother's Love

A Colorful Life

Love & War

* * *

Special Collections & Boxed Sets

From light-hearted comedies to stories about finding hope in the darkest of times, these special boxed editions offer a great way to catch up or to fall in love with Melissa Storm's books for the first time.

Melissa Storm is a mother first, and everything else second. Writing is her way of showing her daughter just how beautiful life can be, when you pay attention to the everyday wonders that surround us. So, of course, Melissa's USA Today bestselling fiction is highly personal and often based on true stories.

Melissa loves books so much, she married fellow author Falcon Storm. Between the two of them, there are always plenty of imaginative, awe-inspiring stories to share. Melissa and Falcon also run a number of book-related businesses together, including LitRing, Sweet Promise Press, Novel Publicity, Your Author Engine, and the Author Site. When she's not reading, writing, or child-rearing, Melissa spends time relaxing at home in the company of a seemingly unending quantity of dogs and a rescue cat named Schrödinger.

GET IN TOUCH!
www.MelStorm.com
author@melstorm.com

Made in the USA
Middletown, DE
31 March 2019